NAME'S CORCORAN, TERRENCE CORCORAN

JOHNNY GUNN

WOLFPACK
PUBLISHING
— EST 2013 —

Name's Corcoran, Terrence Corcoran

Johnny Gunn

Paperback Edition
© Copyright 2018 Johnny Gunn

Wolfpack Publishing
6032 Wheat Penny Avenue
Las Vegas, NV 89122

ISBN: 978-1-64119-113-5

NAME'S CORCORAN, TERRENCE CORCORAN

CHAPTER 1

SOMETHING WOKE HIM UP, NOT WITH A START, JUST something that nudged his senses awake. Listen as he might, all he could hear was – nothing. Snow was softly falling, not driven by winds out of hell; rather, large, downy flakes that drifted gently from a quiet sky. Reminded him of the time he and his little brother got in a pillow fight and ripped one of them open. *My God that was a long time ago. I wonder where that little scamp is now. I was sixteen when I left and he was thirteen.*

Normally Terrence Corcoran would enjoy an opportunity to remember his past, his travels from the filth of New York's docks to the beauty of the Rocky Mountains, and then the bitter fights with Indians as the red men tried desperately to hang on to their way of life. He remembered riding up to the Fetterman massacre and puking for half an hour, and also remembered the good times with some dance hall girls. *In a raging blizzard I don't have time to think, but with snow like this, it's almost like a soft spring rain.*

"There," he muttered. Did he hear something, feel

something? *There was something,* he thought. It must have caught his sleeping attention; something or someone brushed up against a tree or bush and he'd heard the gentle swish of a branch unloaded its frozen cargo of snow. Not gently enough, though, and he slowly brought his trusty Winchester '73, warm and ready to kill, from his bedroll and looked hard toward where he thought he heard the sound.

This long tall man had ridden through the gathering storm most of the day, from near the Carson Sink west to Six Mile Canyon and had finally run out of desire to go any farther about three hours after sunset, when the plug was pulled and the raging winds swept down the canyon, driving raindrops the size of a five-dollar gold piece and just about as heavy. The rain turned to ice within half an hour. The drenched rider tethered old Rube and flung his bedroll under an outcropping of rock, twenty feet or so above Six Mile Creek, which was quickly filling its banks.

His blondish, reddish hair hung in long curls and waves, his eyes, a deep green that generally had humor and mirth writ large, were narrowed into slits determined to find whatever woke him. *My first night back to Virginia City and I've already found trouble. No, Terrence, lad, trouble seems to have found you. Again.*

He wanted to chuckle but held it in, remembering two days ago. That was trouble, and it was etched in his brain. There were two men, either cowboys off one of the local ranches, or looking for work, who walked into the gun shop in Ione. Corcoran was buying some ammunition for his rifle and sidearm when one of the buckaroos shoved him aside, pointed a big Colt at the attendant and demanded the cashbox.

Corcoran stumbled back a step or two from the shove, whipped his Peacemaker out and put two slugs through the cowpoke's chest, turned as a bullet whistled past his head and fanned two more shots at the partner. One nicked him in the shoulder and the other missed giving the partner time to load down on Corcoran.

Corcoran dove for the floor, twisted onto his back before hitting the boards and fired once more, this time putting a neat hole in the man's forehead. He was just getting back to his feet when Sheriff Jackson Clements raced into the gun shop. "What's all this?" he demanded.

Luckily for Corcoran, the shopkeeper, Gus Hines gave a full accounting of the attempted robbery.

"Well, I believe you, Gus," Clements said. "Corcoran, you've just about used up your welcome around these parts. Trouble follows you, I think. It might be best if you drifted on to other diggin's."

"You know dang well this wasn't me starting a fight or nothin', Sheriff." Corcoran complained.

Clements just scowled.

"Alright, then, but at least say thank you for cleanin' up this little hell hole you call home. Probably paper on those two, and if there is, you better forward the bounty my way.

"What do I owe you, Gus?" Corcoran asked.

"Nothing, Terrence. Thanks for stepping in and protecting me." Gus Hines glared at the sheriff. "Some people don't know how to show gratitude, Corcoran. I ain't one of them."

3

———

WHEN THE ICE storm turned to snow, Corcoran gathered several armloads of semi-dried wood, got his knife out and whittled some kindling, rubbed it good with some pork fat, sprinkled some black powder over the little mess, and struck flint. *I can feel that fire all the way to my bones,* he thought, and he let it rage. "No self-respecting Indian would be out in this weather. Way I figger it, I'm pretty darn safe. Safe and cold and wet and damn this storm." This time he said it out loud.

IT WAS NEARING the end of 1884. Christmas was on its way and once again this gentleman wasn't going to be spending it in front of a glowing fireplace surrounded by a loving family. *More'n likely sittin in a mud hole in front of a puny little smoky fire eatin beans and passin' gas. Merry Christmas.*

His camp was at the base of Six Mile Canyon, so Virginia City was about six miles away. Just six miles and he would return to the fabulously rich Comstock Lode. The mine owners, gamblers, and stock market buffoons might be rich, he thought, but he sure wasn't. *Money ain't no problem in Virginia City. It flows like molten gold from that mountain.*

Virginia City was six miles up, a very steep up, at the head of a long climb and he wasn't gonna ride there through a maelstrom that was slinging snow down that long grade. "I'm warm and if Mr. Mackay don't like me not making it through tonight, that's just his tough luck."

Mr. Mackay was John Mackay, owner of the rich Consolidated and California mine that Corcoran thought he might go to work for. Of course, John Mackay had never heard his name mentioned. "So," Corcoran figured, "this storm delay don't mean anything, anyway. One more opportunity lost in this long life of good news/bad news, happy days/ foul days, bonanza/ borrasca. Stuff it, Mr. Mackay, I don't want to work for you, anyway."

That was when he had his camp set up, after he had some jerked meat soaked in hot coffee, and a set-to with more wood for the fire. All that took place before he laid his head on the hard saddle and wrapped himself in a buffalo robe coat and wool bedroll and drifted into a deep sleep.

So, what caused that overladen branch to drop its snow-load, and what was he preparing to kill, wound, or scare half to death with his trusty '73? Corcoran sat rock still, breathing as slow as one can and not pass out, just like old Seth Bullock taught him when he rode for him in Deadwood. *That was back around eighty, I guess. Time ain't caught up with me, no sir, I'm just as fast and deadly as I was then, but I don't like not knowin' what it is trying to kill me.*

There, he heard it again, something rubbed gentle-like against a branch, and right smack in front of him. Snow was flying so thick he couldn't see old Rube and he knew the old caballo was only twenty-feet or so away. There were piñon pine, cottonwood, aspen, and juniper just outside the little cave, but with that big fire going strong in front of the cave, he was having trouble seeing what might be to the other side. *Nice and warm, blind as a bat.*

Corcoran was hunkered down behind a rock, had his finger on the trigger and thumb on the hammer. He always kept a round in the chamber so's he would only have to pull the hammer back, and wouldn't have to take the time to lever a round in. Saved his bacon more than once. Didn't want to pull that hammer back just yet, make enough noise in this stillness to sound like a 4-4-0 highballing across Washoe Valley.

He saw the glint of steel. It had to be the barrel of a handgun. *I cussed that fire a minute ago and now I'm sending the praise out. Glint off steel and you gonna be a dead man.* He eased the Winchester into firing position, tucked tight into his shoulder.

"Want to see sunlight, better let me see you," he hollered, thumbing the hammer back. "Ease your skinny butt out where the light shines bright or die where you sit."

The little speck of bright steel moved up a bit, swung just a degree or two in Corcoran's direction, and he fired, levered, fired, levered, and listened to the horrible sound of a human screaming in mortal pain.

Damn. Hopin' that might have been a nice big buck.

"Damn fool," he muttered, getting to his feet. He added some more big logs to the fire, got a branch burning like a torch, and moved slowly to the patch of brush where the moans and thrashing were coming from. Snow was already deep. "Looks like I was right, just a damn fool. What were you sneaking up on me for, Mr. Lathrop?"

Corcoran carried a badge in Virginia City until he

got all liquored up one night and shot the sheriff. "He didn't much care for that and took my badge away, even as I was doctoring him." Corcoran arrested Mr. Lathrop a couple of times in those days. "Haven't seen you since I left old Virginia Town, Lathrop. Why you sneaking up on me?"

Lathrop was awful busy trying to stay alive, so Corcoran reached down and picked up an old Remmie, eased the hammer down, and tucked it in his belt. "Crawl your skinny butt up to the fire and I'll try to keep you alive, but I really don't know why I'd want to do that. Run you into town in the morning, I might even get my old job back. I don't think the sheriff would hold a grudge this long, no sir, I don't."

Corcoran kept a good fire going and both he and Lathrop slept well. Corcoran got the fire going even more when they awakened and put on some coffee. Then he tended to Lathrop's nasty wound. Bullet went right through the meatiest part of the man's shoulder, tore a chunk out , and busted up the bones that got in the way. Lathrop's arm just hung loose like it wasn't connected to anything.

"Won't be using that arm for some time, Mr. Lathrop. Where's your horse?"

Lathrop nodded off in the direction of the main trail and Corcoran walked out there, actually waddled through two feet of snow, found the cayuse tethered to a tree and brought him into camp, tying him off next to Rube. He laughed out loud watching Lathrop try to pour coffee with his off hand, keep the lid on the pot, and balance a tin cup. It was a mess of the kind that always tickled.

"Ain't never used your left hand for much of anything, eh Mr. Lathrop? I'll fry us up some sidemeat, make a little redeye gravy for the hard tack, and we'll be on our way. Please don't die until I get you to the courthouse."

HIS NAME WAS CORCORAN, Terrence Corcoran, brought to this country from Dublin as a baby, and he'd been on the loose since he was sixteen or so. Corcoran had a brilliant sense of humor, would fight for what's right, to back a friend, or just for the hell of it. His wavy reddish hair hung a bit long most of the time, but he did try to keep shaved. The man was proud of a thick moustache, almost walrus-sized, and his bright green eyes usually shone with warmth and a touch of mirth.

Corcoran lived day to day, he had no plans for tomorrow, could talk himself into a job anytime he felt he needed one. He'd carried a badge in many little towns, burgs, and villages, had spent time in just as many jails, but had no papers spread around with his name and picture prominent. His jail time came from fight time, and he would be the first to tell you, "fightin' ain't a crime, boyo."

There may have been no more than ten saloons between Santa Fe and Boise that didn't know Terrence Corcoran, meaning he was well-known. His word was solid gold and respect came his way from many directions. On the other hand, there were a few detractors among those on the losing side of bar room brawls and one-on-one fights.

———

THE SNOW WASN'T GOING to let up and Corcoran had no desire to spend a day sitting under a rock overhang listening to Lathrop moan and groan. "Okay, Buckey, let's get movin'. Up, fool, up!" he said, kicking the wounded lightly man in the ribs. "Get your horse saddled and bridled."

"Can't do that, Corcoran. Arm won't work," Lathrop moaned. Corcoran kicked snow in the man's face and walked over to dress both horses.

"Get your skinny butt in the saddle or walk," he said, tying off his bedroll and knocking his fire about. Lathrop had a hard time mounting but finally got in the saddle and the two plodded up Six Mile Canyon, through stands of cottonwood and aspen, groves of pine and fields of sage. They had to ford the now boiling Six Mile Creek often as the trail led higher and higher toward Mount Davidson.

"It was at the head of this canyon, Mr. Lathrop, that old Henry Comstock and his pack of whiskey drenched boys discovered that ledge of silver. It's because of that, that Virginia City came to be. Pretty interesting, eh, Mr. Lathrop? Don't you be falling out of that saddle just cuz you think you're runnin' out of blood.

"I won't help you none, no sir, I won't. It was you tried to shoot me, so you just buck up, old man. Old man Locatelli is gonna give me my old tin star back because of you, Mr. Lathrop. Don't you do somethin' dumb like dying or falling off your dumb old horse."

CHAPTER 2

"CORCORAN, YOU NEVER FAIL TO AMAZE ME," SHERIFF
Emilio Locatelli said when Corcoran escorted Lathrop
into his nice warm office in the Virginia City courthouse. Locatelli was almost forty, came to this country
with his parents as a baby, and the family moved to
California during the gold rush years.

Emilio had ditched the family when he was fourteen,
ran with some Mexican outlaws for a few years, and
branched out into the law business when he found out
the Mexicans had rewards on their heads. The reward
kept him alive for some time, he used to say, since
deputies didn't make as much as he felt he needed to
live the good life.

Locatelli moved up and down the Sierra Nevada,
camp to camp, working as a town marshal, a sheriff's
deputy, a city copper, or anything else that let him carry
a badge and make a few bucks on the side, keeping
certain people out of trouble.

Corcoran stood in front of the sheriff's desk, thinking, *Before I shot him, he and I worked well together.*

"Nice to see you, Sheriff," he said, as nicely as he could. "Had a little camp at the bottom of Six Mile when old Lathrop here decided to cash in my chips. Didn't much care for his game so I shot him and I'm bringing him to you instead of just leavin' him out there to bleed all over the good Nevada desert."

Locatelli scrunched his eyes up and brushed hard at his muttonchops, stood up, and Corcoran feared he'd go for that big Colt he liked so much, but instead, he walked around his desk and hit him between the eyes with the biggest fist Corcoran had ever seen comin' straight at him.

Corcoran bounced off most of the furniture in that little office and finally, just kinda spun around and fell face-first onto the bare plank floor, feeling the toe of a boot mashing into a very private place. Later, Corcoran remembered, *I don't think I lost my entire breakfast when everything came up, but then again, well, maybe I did.* County employees on the second floor of that stone courthouse said the howls and groans went on for a full minute.

"Get up, Terry," Locatelli said, sitting back down in his big leather chair that was also a rocker, and that held a little pocket pistol on each side, tucked into the upholstery. Easy to get to those little pop-guns. "Welcome back. No hard feelings, now that we're even?" he asked. Locatelli chuckled as he pulled a big Italian cigar, black and twisted, wine soaked, and more for chewing than smoking, and jammed it between his teeth, and gave the evil eye.

"You look good, Sheriff," Corcoran whimpered. He got to his feet, wiped the blood from his eyes and ears, blew snot into his wildrag, and found his hat, all scrunched up where he had fallen. "It's good to be back. You got a nip back there?" Locatelli found his flask in the bottom drawer on the left side, took a draw for himself, and handed it across.

"I got four deputies, Corcoran. Three here in town and one in Gold Hill. Me and two deputies have the dayshift here in town, and the one in Gold Hill is day shift too. I just appointed you as my undersheriff.

"You take the evening shift, I'll take the day shift. Seven to seven, six days a week." The sheriff said, tossing an old badge across the desk. "Shoot me again and I'll kill you," he smiled, grabbing the flask back. "Where you been?"

"Went up to Austin, over to Belmont, down to Bullfrog, and back to Austin. Got nothing to show for it, so figgered on getting' on one of Mr. Mackay's mines, that is, until Lathrop here wanted to do me in. Yup," he said, "it's nice to be back. I'll put him in a cell and get a doc to look at that shoulder."

"Yeah, Corcoran, you do that. Two dollars a day and you can throw your stuff in the shed behind my house. There's a bench bed in there, too. Don't burn the place down." Locatelli waved his new deputy off and started looking over some papers he had on his desk.

Corcoran's smile told his thoughts. *It just feels nice and warm all over, knowing I have a good job wearin' this old tin badge and making some real money again. Two years is a long time to be gone from a minin' camp, but I guess you can't really call this little metropolis a camp, now, can I?*

Virginia City was decidedly not a mining camp. It was a sophisticated city by any standard, filled with people from every social level. Miners made up the bulk of the population, many from the world's mining centers in Cornwall, Ireland, Germany, and Italy. There were extremes of wealth and poverty, of lawlessness and lawfulness, and education and religion were both well-respected.

The jail was in the basement of the courthouse, virtually escape proof being underground. The walls were solid granite and the steel was bolted right into them. He had to help Lathrop down the narrow stairs and into one of the tiny cells. The man was weak from loss of blood and the manhandling he took on the trip up the canyon. "You have yourself a nice stay, now Mr. Lathrop," Corcoran said.

After Lathrop was tucked in, Corcoran found the doc and sent him scurrying to the jail, and decided to take a spin around the old town. The badge looked good, he thought, walking by one of the shop windows on C Street and catching his image in a window. Corcoran wandered up to the Washoe Club, nodded to a couple of old friends standing at the long bar, and grabbed a cigar out of the box sitting close. He'd been gone from town more than two years and couldn't see that one thing had been moved in the elegant bar from when he left.

Along with the International Hotel, the Washoe Club was a local's place at all hours of the day and night. Powerful mining nabobs, mining engineers, and stock market mavens held sway in both places. The barroom was long and narrow with the bar along the north wall. There were tables along the opposite wall and in the back. At the end of the bar and in the back, gaming tables were set up. Faro was a favorite, along with poker and a couple of dice games.

Virginia City was not a dirty little mining camp. The old town was filled with magnificent Victorian age mansions and homes, gas lamps lit the streets at night, men dressed in the finest of fashion, and their women's clothing came from the finest outlets on the west and east coasts.

"A little whiskey, my friend," Corcoran said to the barman. *This is someone I don't know yet, but will soon enough.* "Hello, Jeb," he said to one of the men he had nodded to. "Looks like you been in a hell of a fight."

Jeb was bandaged and splinted and wrapped just about everywhere, drinking with a bent-up arm that didn't seem to work very well.

"Big old rock slide down on the sixteen hundred level at the Savage Mine," he said. "When'd you get back? Figgered that sheriff'd shoot you on sight," he laughed.

"Naw, me and Locatelli got all that out of the way," Corcoran replied. He immediately thought about that boot toe once again and tried not to. "Anything cookin' that might be interesting to talk about?" Jeb used to run with a bad crowd 'till he learned that it wasn't fun to get caught.

Jeb was some kind of boss at the Savage, now, made more money than he did as a highwayman. Hank Monk took him right out of the saddle on his last job with that big old mule whip of his. Spent a year mopping floors at the courthouse and eatin' slop from one of the whorehouse kitchens. He was following a straight and narrow ledge, and he wanted everyone to believe that.

"Heard about somethin' at the freight office, maybe the Wells Fargo office, can't remember which, but don't know nothing. Locatelli gave you back that old piece of tin you like so much? Never figgered on that," he cackled. Jeb then moved down the bar and sidled up to Corcoran like he wanted to say something, but not for anyone else to hear.

"Pour another whiskey, Corcoran, and let's go set a spell," Jeb said, motioning at a table near the back of the saloon. It sat next to a set of doors that led to a stairway that took the big mucky-mucks up to the Millionaires Hall on the second floor. Had to be a rich dude mine owner or banker to go up those stairs. Most regular men guessed they would never know what that place looked like.

Stories filtered about velvet curtains and teak wood tables, about silver goblets and gold dinnerware, but no one Corcoran knew had really been up there. *Must be some truth to it, though, since the likes of John Mackay and Jim Fair go up there, regular like.*

Men like John Mackay and James Fair spent time there, along with William Sharon, and from time to time the air would be filled with smoke from cigars held by the governor, U.S. Senators, or the elite from San Francisco. Adolph Sutro was said to have his own table, brought in from Germany, and monogrammed silverware.

"You ever heard of Eløn Jaeckes?" Jeb asked as soon as they sat down. "Calls himself a duke or something from somewhere in Europe. Wears all kinds of fancy stuff like velvet jackets and silver studs on big black belts that hold swords and long barrel pistols."

"Sounds like quite the gent, Jeb. Don't reckon I've heard tell of him, though. What kind of name is Eløn?" Corcoran was working on wondering where this conversation might be going.

Jeb answered, "I don't know, Hungary maybe?" he asked.

"No, I ate on the trail," Corcoran said.

"No, Terrence, Hungary is a country in Europe," the stove-up man laughed, and Corcoran almost got riled at him.

"I don't much care to be snickered at. Why would a country be named hungry, anyway?"

"It's part of the Austro-Hungarian kingdom, is what Jaeckes says."

"So, what's this duke guy done?"

"Don't know about what he might have done, but I think he wants to rob the Bank of California, and he's puttin' together a group of men what could almost be an army."

Old Jeb and Corcoran spent another hour discussing this Elon Jaeckes and the gang he was putting together. "What's the sheriff think of all that?"

"Don't know as how the sheriff even knows about it, Terrence. Locatelli isn't the same man you used to work for. With the new district attorney, Locatelli doesn't seem to give much thought to bein' sheriff."

"I'll check that out, Jeb," Corcoran said after about three little glasses of bad whiskey. Corcoran headed down C Street to find something to eat. Most of his breakfast was all over the floor up at the Sheriff's, and despite the lingering pain, he had to chuckle, just a bit.

I've been gone two years and it looks like Virginia City

has grown considerable during that time. There had been a massive fire back in '75, but Corcoran was aware of that. Three quarters of the town burnt to the ground and what he saw was the rebuilding. "Rock and brick, steel and stone," he muttered. He'd never heard such commotion as came from the mine hoisting works, the mills, and the railroad, not to mention the foul language coming from scores of teamsters moving massive wagons through the middle of the city.

Most of the mining towns suffered massive fires, and those that lived on the Comstock rebuilt with brick and concrete, not wood. There were great iron shutters for the doorways and windows in the event of another fire, and often, the attics of conjoined buildings were open to each other.

The old Silver Dollar hotel had a nice little café in the back of the bottom floor. Virginia City was built on the side of a steep old mountain that was filled with high grade silver. The café faced D Street and you had to climb some steep old steps to get to the hotel's main entrance on C Street. The lettered streets ran north and south and the whole town was terraced. C Street was the main street in the town with B and D streets being commercially active as well.

Mines were located along a north-south line, with hoisting works, engineering offices, assay offices, and luxury offices smack in town, the tailing piles growing by hundreds of tons an hour. Boarding houses lined many streets, and C Street was also lined with saloons and gambling parlors, hotels, and major interests such as the Bank of California, the stock exchange, and Wells Fargo and Company.

Corcoran sashayed into the Silver Dollar Café as if he owned the place, and stopped dead at his first glimpse of Susanna O'Meara. She came out of the kitchen and all he could see was a goddess, a vision of loveliness he had never even thought about in his most prurient dreams. Susanna stood almost six feet tall and had all her various parts and pieces in all the right places. The arrangement was perfection and Terrence Corcoran, late of Cork, was in love.

"Hello," she said in a voice any canary would kill for. "I'm Susanna, can I get you a table."

"Uh, yes," he stammered, then remembered his manners. "Name's Corcoran, Terrence Corcoran," he said, doffing his beat up old sombrero and slipping out of his buffalo robe coat. She saw the piece of tin attached to his wool vest and gave him a warm smile, like she was impressed. *Oh, my lord, my lord, what a vision. Be still my heart.*

She had the slightest lilt to her speech, like she hadn't been that many years from the old sod, and that brought memories of Corcoran's ma and pa, and all the uncles and aunts and cousins and even some of the old neighbors along the waterfront. Their brand of the King's English wasn't what he heard most often since coming west many years ago.

Corcoran's mind went into a high lope. *I guess I'm in a dream, kinda, and I can almost smell the green of home. Pa and Ma Corcoran came from Cork, and they tell me I was born two weeks out on the voyage to Boston, so I've never really enjoyed the aroma of the green Isle, but pa sure talked about it a lot. Just listen to this charming lady.*

Susanna broke the reverie by asking if he wanted

coffee. "Coffee would be nice," he said, smiling into brilliant green eyes set in the face of an angel. Her lips were full and seemed to carry a constant smile, her little nose had a distinct upturn, and her flowing deep auburn hair shone as with stardust, as it cascaded about broad shoulders.

"And maybe a platter of meats and bread, darlin'," he said. "I don't understand how it is that we haven't met?" Corcoran said, trying his best to keep her at the table if possible.

"Maybe because it is, Terrence Corcoran, that you haven't been in town for more than two years," a voice boomed from the table behind him. "Miss O'Meara will be joining me for some music and theater tonight at Piper's Opera House, so just behave yourself, old man."

Corcoran whirled about to see just who it was talking like that. "Tin Cup," he yowled. "Tin Cup Duffy. When did they let you out? Oh, I'll find the judge that let that fiend out, so help me, Pa Corcoran, I'll find him."

"Your attempt at gettin' me locked up for one to five went by the boards when you shot the sheriff, old man. Thanky, though. Locatelli gave you your tin-badge back? The man's losin' it, I think."

"Plannin' anymore hijinks like tyin' wagon wheels to water troughs? Or have you finally reached your majority?" Corcoran said, giving Susanna an evil little grin. "He's a naughty boy, Mr. Tin Cup Duffy is."

"Naughty I was, Naughty I'm not," Tin Cup said. "I'd like to talk to you a bit after we dine, Terrence." The deputy could see his eyes darken as he said that and his sly grin disappeared. "'Tis important, old man." Tin Cup had always called everyone 'old man'.

"I'll be makin' my rounds, Tin Cup. You will find me in or near the Sazerac Club about three or so," he said. He turned back to his platter of meats and cheeses, sipped some fine coffee, and delighted in watching Miss O'Meara walk about the café.

"Have you been to one of the fine dances at the Miner's Union Hall?" he asked Susanna as he paid for lunch.

"Oh, my, yes," she said. "Tin Cup has taken me two times, and we danced until I almost couldn't walk," she said, full of life and vigor. Corcoran didn't need to hear any more talk of Tin Cup Duffy and made his way along D Street to the north, turned up to C Street and walked south into the heart of Virginia City.

Virginia City sat on top of the richest single silver lode that had ever been discovered in North America and was home to about twenty thousand souls, some filthy rich, some dirt poor, all looking for their own bonanza. The town had burned to the ground at least once, and most of the buildings were now built of stone, brick, and steel.

The Virginia and Truckee Railroad had relieved some of the heavy traffic that moved south toward Nevada's capitol, Carson City. Mills in town, in Gold Hill, in Silver City, and along the Carson River turned that ore into great ingots of gold and silver. Many of those ingots made their way to the United States Mint in Carson City. The town was a metropolis with elegant hotels, saloons, restaurants, and shops filled with the finest the west coast and Europe could provide.

Women paraded their elegant fashions regularly at performances at Piper's Opera House, performances from the finest Shakespeare companies to song and dance companies. Men in starched white shirtfronts, waistcoats, high top shoes, and silk high hats accompanied them.

Mine owners were proud to tell stockholders that their miners were paid the handsome sum of four dollars per day, one of the highest industrial wages in the world. There were fine schools located in each of the wards, churches stood tall and proud, led by St. Mary's in the Mountains Catholic church.

Corcoran took great pleasure in the city, knew many of the people, Irish, Italian, and Cornish families, almost getting along with each other. He particularly enjoyed the comradeship and arguments that took place between the many fire companies. *This is the liveliest town I've ever lived in, and certainly the biggest.*

CHAPTER 3

AT ONE-TIME, TIN CUP WAS KNOWN AS RICHARD ALLEN White, and he owned part interest in lead within the Savage Mine, which brought him enough funds that he could enjoy life without benefit of extreme labor. As so many before him, he never anticipated the day the lead might play out, that those delightful funds might quit showing up on a regular basis. That day did come, though, and over a period of several weeks, Mr. White was no longer living at Mrs. Borden's Rooms for Gentlemen, and found himself slopping hogs for Adolph Sutro in Sutro City along the Carson River.

White was a miner, not a hog-slopper, he told himself daily. He finally found himself in possession of a ten-dollar gold piece, a well-used bedroll, a tin cup, and came back to the Comstock, not the nabob he preferred being, but able to hold his head up.

The trip was memorable in that he rode the four and a half miles up the Sutro Tunnel in an empty ore cart pulled by a mule. The destination was the seventeen-hundred-foot level of the Savage mine, that is, seventeen hundred feet below C Street, Virginia City.

He rode a man-cage to the surface, doffed his bowler to the hoistman, and wandered down the Queen City of the Comstock's main artery of commerce. He then sidled up to the bar at the Washoe Club. With a bit of a flourish, he laid the tin cup on the bar and said, in a firm voice, "Fill 'er up, mate." Thus, the legend of Tin Cup began.

To say the man's wick wasn't furnished with the best oil would be a good guess. He wanted to be a gambler but his mind simply wasn't quick enough to put two and two together and come up with four. He tried his hand at carpentry, but the philosophy of "close enough" doesn't work in that game either. He had lowered himself to a lesser denominator and was often found drunk and disorderly.

Over a period of years, Tin Cup was known as a double-dealer, a drunken fool, a man with the heart of a larcenist, and a wanna-be mining nabob. Corcoran knew, without a doubt, that Tin Cup was involved in many of the small-time robberies that happened around the area, but was never quite able to nab him.

I don't think I understand what appeared on the surface during our meeting at the café with the blustering fool. What was I hearing him trying to say? In Corcoran's mind, the entire scene at the café was unsettling at best. *I'm not his friend, don't want to be his friend, and I better keep my wits about me.*

Tin Cup seemed to have a clean, well-fitting suit of clothes on that foul body, had money enough to squire that charming lady about town, and wanted to meet with the deputy. "Ah, Terrence, my friend," he mumbled softly, "beware, beware."

It was a cold and blustery evening on the Comstock as Corcoran walked about the streets. He stuck his head in many of the businesses that were still open as he walked down the length of C Street. He'd been gone for some time and renewed acquaintances in some, ducked insults in others, and offered threats to some. He had just arrived back after spending a couple of years in mining camps and ranches that weren't quite as sophisticated as Virginia City, and was marveling at the way people dressed.

"Corcoran, in here, be quick about it," a man waved to him from the front of Shipley's Golden Spur Saloon. The big deputy raced across C Street an into the dingy smoke-filled saloon, and smack into a melee. At least three men were going at it, two with knives and one with an oak stave. Corcoran ducked as the stave was swung at his head, pulled his big Colt Peacemaker and put another hole in the ceiling.

"That's enough, boys, break it up!" He whacked the guy with the stave, saw the two with knives slip the sharp steel into scabbards, and nodded at the group. "Who did what? One at a time, starting with you," he said, pointing at one of the knife men.

"Just wanted a drink, Terrence. Didn't know the man bought the whole damn bottle. All he had to do was say no. Pulled that damn knife on me." Rusty Melancon had a slight scrape on his cheek and Corcoran looked at the other knife man.

"Your bottle?" The man nodded. "Why didn't you just say no?"

The man shrugged and poured a shot. "Damn fool. Next time, take your bottle to a table so's others will know."

He looked at the man with the stave. "Well?"

"Just protectin' my territory," he whimpered. A big welt was forming where Corcoran had whacked him.

"Bunch of idiots," Corcoran bellowed. "Drink nice or go to jail. Don't make me come back in here!" He tucked the Colt back in its holster, glared at the surrounding bunch and walked out the door. *It's nice to be back home.*

One could tell the miner getting off shift. He looked haggard and beat down after spending ten hours deep in the bowls of this old earth, breathing foul air, facing extreme temperatures from the scalding fissures of an active geothermal system that plagued the Comstock mines.

Gentlemen stock brokers and bankers strode along the boardwalks with their carved walking sticks and jaunty silk high hats, and elegant ladies in the fashions of Paris and London looked down their lovely noses at those not as well-heeled.

At the corner of C and Taylor he slipped into the Sazerac Club, kitty-corner from the Bank of California. The bank was a strong, brick building, two full stories tall, with what was reported to be a massive vault that simply couldn't be attacked with file, hammer, or dynamite.

William Sharon was the manager, and he was boastful at times about the fact that his bank had never been successfully robbed, despite a few who had tried. Sharon manipulated many of the mining interests, was heavily involved in many mills along the Carson River, and was a part of the management and ownership of the Virginia and Truckee Railroad.

Directly across C Street from the bank was the Wells Fargo offices in an equally strong brick building. Many of the structures in Virginia City were all but brand new as a massive fire, back in 1875 burned most of the town to the ground. The old wooden structures were tinder dry in the high-altitude air, and the flames could be seen in Carson City, fifteen miles away.

"A pint of your finest ale, Michael," he said to the proprietor, Michael Donahue, a retired lawman. The Sazerac was a small saloon, long and narrow, with a few tables along the south wall and the bar stretching out along the north wall. Unlike many of the thirst parlors, the Sazerac did not offer any gaming tables nor did it have any working girls. Donahue liked to say he wanted his patrons to fully enjoy the pleasures of a fine drink, which shouldn't be interrupted by such shenanigans as gambling and wicked women.

He allowed no shenanigans in his establishment and kept the peace by way of a ten-gauge fowling piece, and the bulk of well over two hundred pounds. His family had arrived from Ireland way back in the 1600s, but the flavor of those misty isles never left Michael.

"So, Terrence, you got that tin badge back, did you? I suppose Sheriff Locatelli forgave you?"

"In a manner of speaking, yes," Corcoran said, still feeling the ache between his legs, and the swelling knot on his head. "Tin Cup said he wanted to meet with me, Michael. You wouldn't have any idea why, would you?"

Tin Cup was refused service in several of the saloons up and down C Street, but Donahue usually let him have at least one or two before suggesting that he drink somewhere else.

"Have you met our new District Attorney, Ezra McNabb, Terrence?" Donahue asked, pouring a second pint for the deputy. He seemed to ignore the question about Tin Cup.

"What happened to Dibitanto?"

"Run out on a rail while you were on your little vacation. Found with his fingers in the pie, laddy. Also found in the wrong bed one morning. Dibitanto wasn't a bad district attorney, but his wasn't the wisest of minds, either.

"McNabb has an interesting group of acquaintances, Corcoran, including Tin Cup White, or as he prefers these days, Tin Cup Duffy."

"I've heard another name, Michael. Elon Jaeckes. Jeb Miner gave me a hint that he might be involved in some interesting happenings around town."

"There are others, and there are plans afoot that I have heard rumblings about, but nothing rock-solid. The outlaw group in town has grown some while you were gone, and Locatelli doesn't have a handle on it. Rumor is, McNabb has something on the sheriff, enough of something, to put a gag on Locatelli's actions."

For the second time since returning to Virginia City, Corcoran had heard about some kind of outlaw society building in the town, and now it seemed that both the district attorney and the sheriff were involved in some way. *I hope I don't have to shoot that man again.*

He chuckled, and looking up saw Tin Cup come into the drinking palace, twirling his little cup by its handle.

"Corcoran, glad you're here. Let's take a table by the front, shall we? And, Michael, could you top this off for me?" he said, handing over the bent up old tin cup. "I, for one, am glad you're back Terrence. You're a good man."

Corcoran wondered where that kind of talk might be coming from. *Tin Cup is thinking I'm some kind of good man? Put yourself in the awareness harness, old man, this fool is up to something.* "Well, thank you, Tin Cup, I've always felt that way myself. What's on your mind?"

"As I recall, Terrence, you have been open to making a double eagle on the side from time to time."

"Aye, laddy, I have, if it's on the proper side of the law's ledger."

"I'm acquainted with a gentleman from Europe who is in need of information, and he is willing to pay a fair price for such information," Tin Cup said. His eyes darted about the narrow saloon as if he might find someone listening in to his prattle.

Corcoran looked about, wondering what or who Tin Cup was be expecting to see.

"There's no one here but us, White. Get on with it." Corcoran loved theatrics as much as any Irisher, but this was getting boring.

"I prefer being Tin Cup Duffy, nowadays, Terrence. So, this European gentleman, did I mention he is from one of the royal families? - is looking for information that someone like you would have. I'm in a position to make the introduction, if you would like."

"I assume this introduction would come at a cost?" Corcoran could almost feel the man's grubby hands deep in his pockets. "I can't imagine what kind of information I might have that anyone else in town might not have. Would we be talking about Elon Jaeckes?"

"Yes, we would," Tin Cup said. "Have you already met the fine gentleman?"

"No, only heard the name. He wears velvet? This is a mining town, not gay Paree. Tell me about this information I might possess and that he desires." The conversation with Jeb Miner was working its way back to the front of Corcoran's mind and what Donahue said about the new district attorney was filtering through as well.

"I can't answer for the duke, Terrence," Tin Cup said. "What I can do is offer you the opportunity of meeting with him. He'll be dining at the International Hotel this evening and I can arrange for you to join him."

"Why don't you do that, Tin Cup. I'd like to meet this so-called duke of yours. Breaking bread with the gentry has always fascinated me. Please inform the gentleman that I'll be wearing what I have on at this very moment as my velvets seem to be missing." He was the only one at the table chuckling as Tin Cup frowned, turned, and stomped out of the saloon.

"Must have said something to irritate the man," Donahue said when Corcoran stepped back to the bar.

"Wants me to meet with that Jaeckes feller tonight. Seems as though the duke wants information that only someone like me would have. Sounds a bit off to me, old man." He took a long draught on his mug of beer and slid the empty across for a refill.

"Did I tell you I brought old Lathrop in this morning? Fool tried to kill me last night."

"He's been running with Tin Cup and might be part

of the group that runs with McNabb's people. Anybody besides you knew you were coming back to town?"

Donahue was pretty sharp and the question caught Corcoran by surprise.

"Well now, Michael, I better give some thought to that. Interesting."

CHAPTER 4

THE COURTHOUSE STOOD TALL AND HANDSOME ON B Street, its heavy stonework and Victorian elegance shone in sunrise terracotta. There was an impressive statue of Lady Justice, un-blindfolded, guarding the entranceway. On the south side of the main floor was the district attorney's offices, and on the north side was the sheriff's claim. Ezra McNabb was a tall, rail thin man of some forty years, with heritage dating back to the original Irish immigrants arriving on the east coast during the 1700s.

He arrived in Virginia City just as the city was learning how District Attorney Dibitanto had been spending county money on a lovely lady who just happened to be married to someone else, and led the charge to oust the fiend from public office. Few questioned his bona fides, just assumed that a man would not call himself an attorney unless he really was one. As one C Street gent was heard to say, "I wouldn't want to be called one."

McNabb came across as a man without a sense of

humor; a fellow who rode a white horse and carried a sharp lance. He was known to change the subject when people started talking about backgrounds and personal histories, and was a frequent dinner guest of one Hungarian Duke, currently residing at the International Hotel.

"Good morning, Donald," he said to his secretary. "Cold this morning. Let's get that fire cooking. You know I can't tolerate cold. Why must I have to say this? Don't force me to make adjustments, Donald."

"Yes, sir," the young man said, scurrying to find more coal to throw in the large pot belly stove in the DA's office. *It's bloody near eighty degrees in here now,* he fumed. *Wear a sweater, old man.* Donald Ferguson was twenty-five-years-old, had come west as a youngster with his parents who lived in Sacramento. McNabb was under the impression that Ferguson hoped to be able to finish his clerking with McNabb and pass the bar, becoming a full-fledged attorney. The district attorney would never believe the truth if it came to be known.

"I passed a man walking down the street wearing a deputy's badge. I don't believe I've ever seen him before. Find out who he is, Donald." McNabb settled in behind his large desk and opened some files that Ferguson had left for him. "I don't like the idea of Locatelli hiring people without letting me know."

The district attorney and the sheriff were elected officials of Storey County and were independent of each other on the books, but McNabb took the position that his office was higher than Locatelli's, and demanded that the sheriff keep him advised of his actions. Maybe Jeb Miner and Michael Donahue were right in thinking that McNabb had something on the sheriff.

"His name is Corcoran, Terrence Corcoran, and he was a deputy a couple of years ago, sir. He just arrived back in town and Sheriff Locatelli hired him back." There were other things Ferguson might have told McNabb, but decided this wasn't the time. *I really like Mr. Corcoran and I'm glad he's back. McNabb and he won't have much in common, I'm afraid.*

"Corcoran brought old Orin Lathrop in this morning. Seems Lathrop tried to shoot him last night. Lathrop's down at the hospital now. Got his arm all messed up."

"Lathrop. Damn fool. Go find Jaeckes. I need to see him right away. Should be at the International. Hurry, damn it."

Ferguson bristled but knew he dare not show it, and pulled himself into his heavy winter coat for the short walk to the International. The International Hotel was elegance personified, standing a full five stories high, it even boasted an elevator, something unique in western mining towns.

Virginia City was home to millionaires by the score, with mines belching silver and gold by the ton almost daily. The builders and financiers from San Francisco flocked to the Queen of the Comstock, gambled on mining stock, ate oysters, and drank champagne from Comstock silver goblets. Ferguson found Jaeckes in a dining parlor on the mezzanine floor.

"Excuse me, sir," he said, still in slight awe over the possibility the man might be of European royalty. "Mr. McNabb would like to see you in his office as soon as possible." Ferguson almost bowed his way away from the table but was called back.

"Wait," the duke commanded. "Did Mr. McNabb say why I should leave my table?"

"A man named Lathrop was arrested this morning, sir. It seems to have upset the district attorney."

"As well it should have. Tell McNabb I'll see him in my suite in one hour." He simply waved a hand, dismissing the law clerk.

Ferguson found that interesting. *McNabb wants Jaeckes in his office pronto and Jaeckes says fine, but in my suite at such and such a time.* Ferguson muttered something about powerful people with no manners.

Ferguson made his way back down B Street to the courthouse. *I don't believe I would do well in Europe. Arrogance like that needs a good thumping. Old pappy used to say you should treat your fellow man the way you wished to be treated. Well, Sir Duke, I would like that chance.* He at least had a smile on his face when he gave the message to McNabb.

McNabb was almost as arrogant as Jaeckes and almost bit the end off his cigar when Ferguson did not produce the duke. He sat at his desk, grumbled, stood up and stormed around the office for a few rounds, demanded more coal be put in the stove, and finally donned his suit coat and overcoat and left the building. Ferguson thought something along the lines of- rude is as rude does.

"You have yourself a wonderful day, Mr. McNabb," Ferguson said, after the man had made his way out of the courthouse. "Don't hurry yourself back," he snickered. *I'm going to be a fine attorney one day soon, and if I ever act that way toward those that work for me I hope they throttle me good.*

EMILIO LOCATELLI MADE his way down the busy main drag of the fabulous city, riding his Arabian stallion, sitting as tall as the squat man could, tipping his hat to the ladies, scowling at those he considered the lower class, and rode south to the Washoe Club. It would be a late dinner in the upstairs Millionaires Club for the sheriff. He tethered Sir Knight and made his way into the busy saloon.

"Well, Jeb Miner. Looks like you're feeling better. That was a nasty accident."

"It was, Sheriff," Miner said. "I see that Corcoran is back in town. Glad to see him back, and I'm glad you gave him his badge back."

"Humph," Locatelli managed. "We'll see how long he can keep it. I don't suppose you've seen Sharon or Mackay go upstairs, have you?"

Miner smirked at the question. The sheriff was not known to mingle with the manager of the Bank of California or with the owner of the richest mine on the Comstock.

"I haven't seen anyone go up today," he managed to get out without a snicker. "I hear that Corcoran was almost shot by that idiot Lathrop. Is Lathrop still working for our local duke?"

"He's just part of the D Street scum. Corcoran shot him up good, though." The sheriff nodded goodbye and went up the steep stairs to the Millionaires Club. It was membership by invitation, based on the amount of mining stock one owned or the number of mines one operated. Elected officials of the county were given honorary membership, something Locatelli enjoyed immensely.

He found the dining room empty and stood at the long bar, all by himself for just a minute, turned, and went back down the stairs, out to the street, mounted his horse, and rode back to the courthouse, frustrated at not being able to rub shoulders with Virginia City's elite. He stuck his nose in the district attorney's office.

"Where's McNabb?"

"I believe he's with Mr. Jaeckes, Sheriff. Something I can help you with?" Ferguson started to stand and offer the sheriff a seat. Instead, Locatelli huffed once, shut the door and left the building. *He's almost as strange as McNabb*, Ferguson chuckled to himself. *Must be something in the water.*

JAECKES WAS RENTING a suite of rooms on the third floor of the International Hotel and had a man-servant and maid on his personal staff. The suite's main room was a reception area with one bedroom changed into an office for the duke. The man-servant was a black man from somewhere in north Africa. His speech was decidedly British, and the man stood almost seven feet tall.

"M'Toobie," Jaeckes said, walking into the main room. "I'm expecting Ezra McNabb. When he arrives show him in, please." M'Toobie's name in fact was almost impossible to pronounce the way he did, and it always came out M'Toobie by everyone else. "Have we heard from that mongrel, Tin Cup?"

"No, Sahib. Would you like a brandy?"

"That and my pipe. If Tin Cup arrives while McNabb is here, get rid of him, otherwise, let me know and I'll see him out here. Not in my office." Jaeckes walked into his office, slipped out of his fine purple velvet suit coat and sat behind his desk. His English was heavily accented most of the time, but not when alone with M'Toobie. At those times, the man sounded like he might be from Boston's waterfront.

His brandy was about half drank when M'Toobie announced Ezra McNabb. "Hello, Ezra," Jaeckes said, standing and offering a hand. "Have a seat. Brandy?" McNabb nodded yes and took a seat in a fine leather covered, hand carved mahogany chair. "I understand you wanted to discuss the plight of Orin Lathrop."

"I do," McNabb snapped. "It seems he tried to shoot a man last night and instead got shot himself. Why was he trying to shoot the man? I have been told that the man he was trying to kill is now a deputy sheriff.

"I don't appreciate all this taking place without my knowledge, Jaeckes. We are supposed to be partners, and I demand answers. We're looking at something that will allow us to live like the mining nabobs if we can pull it off. If you're trying to work around me you'll die, hard and slow, Jaeckes."

"Take it easy, McNabb," Jaeckes said. "Lathrop is almost as ignorant as Tin Cup and saw an opportunity last night. He misjudged the target. It seems that Terrence Corcoran was a deputy here a couple of years ago and was returning when Lathrop thought he had a chance to get some easy money. I have never heard of this Corcoran fellow and certainly did not suggest that Lathrop shoot him.

"I'm looking forward to meeting this Corcoran, though," Jaeckes continued. "I heard that he shot Locatelli once," and he laughed loud at that. "And he's got a reputation as being a bit on the wild side. He would be able to keep us advised on certain information we will need." There wasn't the slightest touch of an accent in his speech.

"What kind of information would a deputy have that I wouldn't have?" McNabb asked, getting his dander up once again.

"The railroad or express company might inform the sheriff's office of certain traffic that they wouldn't necessarily find reasonable to inform the district attorney. We will need some of that information and Corcoran might be able to supply it.

"All right, then. I hoped it was something simple like that," McNabb said. He tossed back the rest of his brandy and indicated he would like some more. "Let's talk about how we can carry this project off. The amount of money involved is more than either of us has ever contemplated. Do we have enough people? Enough men good with guns?"

"That we have, Ezra. What we are lacking right now is dates and times, for one thing, and a means of escape. There are four routes out of Virginia City and all four lead to problems. Toll Road north leads to Reno. Jumbo leads to Washoe. Gold Hill, Silver City leads to Dayton, and Six Mile leads to Sutro. Nothing leads to wilderness, which is what we need.

"Those crates will be filled, Ezra, and heavy. We'll

need a large wagon with at least four-up to haul it off. And the men on that wagon must be professional teamsters and as trustworthy as possible." He shook his head. "What I've found is scum like Lathrop and this fool Tin Cup. The men in Virginia City make too much money, Ezra. In Chicago finding men willing to pull a heist of this size would be a cinch."

SEVERAL OF THE major mines on the Comstock tried paying their men with company script and that lasted less than one full pay period. An attempt at using paper money also failed the test, the men demanding their pay in gold coin. Those double eagles looked and felt so good when they were at the bottom of a pocket or purse.

It was ironic in a way. The men were paid with the same gold they ripped from Mother Earth. The ore they mined was transported by railroad to mills along the Carson River where it was turned into ingots of pure gold and silver. Those ingots in turn were sold to the government and transported to the U.S. Mint in Carson City where they were stamped into coins of the realm.

Those coins were then transported back to Virginia City where they were used to pay the men their wages. Jaeckes and Company were looking to interrupt that cycle just before the last tick. Jaeckes could see that it was one thing to successfully steal the crates of gold and silver coins, it was an entirely different matter to get the loot out of town with the same success.

"What I see, McNabb is one big problem. When that shipment is hit, within moments the telegraph will spread the word to the four corners of the world. We won't be able to get away far enough, fast enough, to be safe."

The meeting was interrupted by M'Toobie. "Tin Cup has arrived, sir," he said.

"Tell him I'm busy and to come back in an hour. He doesn't need to know that McNabb is here."

M'Toobie closed the door and Jaeckes continued. "It would be best, I think, if we had somewhere very close where we could drive the team and hide the wagon. Let's work on that and anything else that might help us. I want Tin Cup to bring me this Corcoran fellow, Ezra, so we can get those schedules. We can't trust Locatelli any longer."

"I agree on everything you've said, Jaeckes. I want to work toward letting the sheriff get the blame for this. Let him take the rap and we take the gold." The meeting ended on that high note, and Ezra McNabb decided not to even bother returning to his office. He headed for the sumptuous saloon downstairs.

CHAPTER 5

A CITY AS LARGE AND WEALTHY AS VIRGINIA WOULD, OF course, have had a district set aside for pleasure of the prurient kind, and that was located along D Street, one level below the main drag. There was a line of small cabins, often referred to as cribs, where the ladies of the night conducted their business. The women were very much a part of the town's flavor and history, many of them wearing elegant gowns to performances at Piper's Opera House.

Terrence Corcoran took a walk down Union Street, one of the steeper grades in town, and turned north on D Street. He popped his head into several of the cribs to say hello, let the ladies know he was back in town, got many hugs and kisses from them, and a few offers.

He had to suggest that a couple of drunks, miners off-shift and playful, should go on home and sleep it off. The officials in town were a bit protective of their working girls and Corcoran was as well. *We must remember they all have mothers and family remembrances. I*

look at them, some of them, as sisters I never had. The others
as lonely ladies who need a friend.

"Hello, my little dove," he said, slipping into Claire Donnegan's crib. "Have you missed your Terrence?" She leaped from the couch she was draped across and flew into his arms.

"Where have you been? You just rode out, didn't say goodbye or nothing. And now, Terrence Corcoran, what? You think you can just ride right back into my arms and my bed?"

"Seems a bit likely to me," he smiled. He eased her back a bit to get a better look at her. "I think you've become even more beautiful, my little one. There have been some changes in the old town, eh?"

"Indeed, Terrence. There's a nasty bunch that have formed and they think they can just do whatever they please. That miserable Tin Cup Duffy and Orin Lathrop are the worst."

"I've brought you a present, Claire, all the way from Bullfrog, Nevada." He reached deep in his buffalo robe coat pocket and brought a small box out. "See if you like this."

She gasped in delight when she lifted the top off the box. "Oh, dear me," she said, over and again. "It's beautiful." She held a gold chain holding a gold shamrock that featured a small diamond in the center. "Terrence, this is beautiful. I'll wear it for the rest of my life." She got serious for a minute. "You didn't steal it, did you?"

He laughed long and hard and she didn't notice that he never quite answered the question. "Soon as I saw it, I had to get it for you, sweet Claire. If I run away again, maybe I'll just see to it that you run with me." He grew thoughtful and asked, "What do you know about Tin Cup and Lathrop? What are they up to?"

"Lathrop is a thief, Terrence, and Tin Cup helps him. Another one of them is that Clarence Boyington. There has been lots of jewelry that's been coming up missing, and Lathrop brags about not having to work, that he's self-employed now. He's very dangerous."

"I shot him last night," Corcoran said. Claire was surprised at how casually he said that.

Claire was a tall, lithe woman of about thirty years, the ravages of a hard life just beginning to make themselves known. If she had a background of note, no one knew about it, none knew of parents or siblings, schools or marriages. What they knew was a still beautiful woman who was expert at her profession.

"I've heard stories about Tin Cup. Old Lathrop tried to kill me and I shot him good," Corcoran chuckled. "Who else is running with them?"

"Clarence Boyington is one and that big man at the brewery."

"Smithson? Ike Smithson is running with Tin Cup and Lathrop? That's a surprise. Keep your pretty little ears open for me, darlin'," Corcoran said. "There's mischief about to take place and I'm not sure who the bad guys are."

It was several hours later that Corcoran made his way to the International Hotel and his late supper meeting with Elon Jaeckes. The smile came natural as he said hello, shook hands with the royal duke, and sat down.

"Tin Cup tells me you've been friends for some time, Mr. Corcoran," Jaeckes said.

"We've been acquaintances, sir. I'm a little pickier about who my friends are. He said you needed some information that I might have. What would that be, and keep in mind that I am an officer of the law. Tin Cup has been known to work outside those confines from time to time."

Jaeckes eyes narrowed a bit as he settled back in his chair. He seemed to be thinking hard about something and didn't take his eyes away from Corcoran. He apparently came to some kind of conclusion, and spoke quietly. "I was under the impression that Mr. Duffy had informed you of my desires."

"Tin Cup likes to give the impression that he knows something you might not know, and then wants to hold that information back and not let you in on something very important. He loves to imply that he knows someone else's secret. He only said you might need some information I might have, and you would be willing to pay for it."

Jaeckes sat quietly, not saying anything, contemplating the tall, well-built deputy standing at his table. Corcoran waited for his answer which, so far, wasn't forthcoming.

"I can't imagine what that information might be since I've been gone for some time and just got back to town. I believe we're both wasting our time, Mr. Jaeckes. Good evening." Corcoran stood up, nodded slightly, and walked out of the dining room. *I think I'll find Mr. Tin Cup Duffy and slap him up across the side of the head. Maybe twice. I wonder what that was all about?*

What would I know that others might not? And important enough that someone might pay for it?

Jaeckes was having the same thoughts, wondering why Tin Cup didn't tell the deputy what would be expected of him, or what would be needed from him. *Tin Cup assured me that this man could be bought for just a few double eagles.*

THE SOUTH END of Virginia City; before reaching what is called The Divide, where Virginia City ends and Gold Hill began, was filled with vile and filthy little gambling parlors and saloons, gaudy in some respects, just dirty and dim in others. The down and out, the criminal or wanna-be criminal element, and the gambling sharks prevailed. Corcoran knew most of them and made it a policy to poke his nose in each place on every round of the town.

"Looky here, boys," the barman piped up as Corcoran entered one of the saloons. "It's the man that shot the sheriff and he's still wearin' a badge. You drinkin', Corcoran or just takin' up room?"

"Just passing through, Bucky. Seen Tin Cup?"

"Duff don't come in here, much. You plannin' to shoot Locatelli again?" That brought laughs from most of the men in the bar. Corcoran laughed with them, didn't say yay or nay, and walked through the heavy smoke and foul air, looking at those at the gambling tables, drinking tables, and standing at the bar.

"You boys have a good night," he said. When he stepped through the bat wing doors he was quietly hailed by a slight man, standing off in the shadows between two buildings. "Sam Owens, is it?"

"Yes, Terrence. I'm glad you're back in town. I don't come into this section of town but I caught sight of you. I need to talk with you, alone."

Owens worked as chief clerk for Wells Fargo, stood barely five-feet-six, weighed under one twenty, was balding and spindly. "There's something going on that you need to know about."

"Let's take a walk down Flowery Street to D Street and then back north and you can tell me all about it," Corcoran said.

They passed the main office complex of the California and Consolidated Virginia Mining Company, that rich complex owned by John Mackay and company, and Owens told Corcoran a grand story.

"I was called to have a meal with Elon Jaeckes yesterday, Terrence. He has offered to pay me a lot of money if I would keep him informed of incoming shipments from the mint in Carson City. Why would he want that? Why would he pay me for that information?"

Corcoran snickered at the man's lack of insight. "Well, Sammy boy, give it just a minute's thought, would you? If you might be plannin' on interrupting one of those shipments it would be good to know the schedule, don't you think?"

Sam Owens stood, thunder-struck. "He's planning on hijacking a shipment? Oh, no." The little man was horrified at the thought, even more so at the thought of him being involved.

"You didn't tell him anything, did you?" Corcoran asked. He was now beginning to understand what

Jaeckes was going to ask him about. *Jaeckes knows that I would know the shipping schedules also. Maybe I walked out on him too soon.* "Tell me, Sam Owens, just what did you and this duke character decide, because I may have an idea for you to think about."

"I told him I'd give it some thought and he shoved five double eagles across the table at me. He said that would be just the down payment on a large payday if I would help him. I don't like this, Terrence. It scares me."

"It should, Sam. If you're up to it, go along with him, but don't ever tell him the truth. You've confided in me and that already puts you in jeopardy with that gang. I suggest you also confide in your superiors in Carson City and tell them what you told me."

Sam Owens drifted off into the shadows and Corcoran continued his walk around the old town, deep in thought. *I've come home to a nest of gangsters, I do believe. I think it's time to get a bit rowdy.*

THE SUN WAS STREAMING up Six Mile Canyon, silhouetting Sugar Loaf when Corcoran walked into the office. "Long day," he said, stuffing coal into the potbelly. He had the office warm, coffee boiling, and his overnight report written for the sheriff when Locatelli walked in.

"So, first night shift and you didn't shoot anyone, eh?" Locatelli was looking over Corcoran's report. "I meant to leave you a note. The district attorney wants to see you. Don't take any crap off that gentleman. I'm the elected sheriff and you work for me. Got it?"

"Yup. I heard some rumors that he's involved with

this Elon Jaeckes feller. Met Jaeckes last night. Seems to have his fingers in things."

"Does that," the sheriff said. "Just between us, I don't think he's who he says he is, and that giant of a servant he has is damn dangerous."

"Guess I didn't meet him."

"He's about seven feet tall and heavy as an ox. Wears fancy silk pantaloons and vests, and I swear he could pick up a building if he felt like it. Don't mess with that one, Corcoran, unless you have a scattergun at hand." Corcoran could almost feel tension as Locatelli spoke.

He's afraid of something or someone. The DA? Surely, he isn't afraid of me. We got that all settled, I think. I need to know more about this McNabb feller. He was amused by the description of the man-servant.

Corcoran remembered stories his father told about Arabs and huge black slaves, and almost got a smile. "I'll keep my eyes open," he said.

They sat and drank coffee and talked about things that neither one was really interested in until the DA opened his office and Corcoran walked across the courthouse lobby to say hello.

"Mornin'," he said to Donald Ferguson. "Understand the man wants to see me."

"Good morning to you, Terrence Corcoran. Glad you're back. I'll tell Mr. McNabb you're here." He scurried into the DA's inner office and right back out. "Come in, Terrence," he said, holding the door open.

"Thankee," he said. "Do you always stoke up the fire like this? Whew, it's hot."

"McNabb is cold-blooded, I think," Ferguson chuckled.

"Mornin', McNabb. I'm Corcoran. Terrence Corcoran. What can I do for you?"

"My name is *Mr.* McNabb, Deputy Corcoran," he said. "I understand you've been asking questions about Duke Elon. He's a fine upstanding citizen and there's no reason for you to question him. You'll cease immediately."

"Sorry if I ruffled feathers, McNabb," Corcoran said, a slight smile playing about his eyes. "By the way, it's *Undersheriff* Corcoran. It is my job, though, and if the sheriff suggests that I not know what's going on in town, maybe I won't ask so many questions.

"Anything else, while I'm here?" Corcoran grinned and at McNabb's stiff silence, he turned and started for the door. The D.A. scowled but said nothing.

Ferguson had been standing just outside the door listening to the conversation, a grand smile across his mug. *Give it to him, Terrence,* he almost said out loud. He was back behind his desk by the time Corcoran walked out of McNabb's office.

"Well, Donald, have you been studying while I've been gone? The way my life plays about, I might just need a good lawyer one day," he chuckled.

Corcoran thought about having breakfast at the Silver Dollar Restaurant and decided he was too tired and would fall asleep in the gravy for sure. He found the shack behind the sheriff's house, slipped out of his boots, hung his gun belt over the bedpost, and flopped down fully-dressed. *I haven't closed my eyes since yesterday morning when I shot old Lathrop.*

After sleeping on the ground for several nights, the cot felt good, a bit lumpy here and there, but even that was better than rocks and twigs. He had visions of Claire Donnegan and Suzanna O'Meara, all mixed up with some duke in purple velvet bloomers dancing with Tin Cup, and was snoring within seconds of his head hitting a mashed-up pillow.

CHAPTER 6

THERE WAS NO QUESTION THAT IT WAS MID-WINTER HIGH in the craggy Virginia Range. The temperature hung near the zero mark, winds blew at gale velocity, reminding the old-timers on Sun Mountain that when they'd arrived, they named these winds Washoe Zephyrs. Never doubt a hard rock miner's sense of humor. Sam Owens was making his way down the boardwalks of Virginia City's main artery, hanging onto anything handy to keep from being blown away.

Winter storms in western Nevada boiled out of the Gulf of Alaska and carried the bitter cold of the Arctic mixed with plenty of moisture. At more than six thousand feet above sea level, Virginia City was often blanketed in snowfall measured in feet, not inches. "Sometimes I need to carry rocks in my pockets, or a long tether," Owens griped.

"Easy there, Sam," Michal Donahue said, stepping onto the walk from his Sazerac Saloon. "One slip on this ice and you'll be blown all the way down the mountain. We'll have to send the posse to find you all scrunched up in the brush down at Sutro's tunnel." He ushered the frail man into the saloon, both of them chuckling on the one hand, and understanding the truth of the situation on the other.

"How about a hot brandy, Mr. Owens? In fact, sir, I'll make two of them, now that I've brought it up." Donahue got busy and Owens made himself as comfortable as he could, nesting close to the potbelly stove that was almost red-hot. "Brandy it is, for two of Washoe's finest."

"Terrence Corcoran and I had a long talk last night, Michael," Sam Owens said. "He suggested that I have almost the same talk with you." His demeanor had changed dramatically, from humor to serious stuff. "It's about Elon Jaeckes."

"Now just what would the Wells Fargo chief clerk have to do with the dubious duke?" Donahue came around from behind the bar with two steaming mugs of coffee and brandy, and settled in at Owens' table. He brought a bottle of brandy along as well.

Donahue's background included a stint with the Army of the Potomac back in the '60s, working as a spy. He mostly worked to find rebel conspirators within the union forces, and was very good at it. Corcoran was among the few along the Comstock Lode that knew that, and often called on Donahue's abilities.

"Corcoran thinks that Jaeckes might be planning to rob one of our shipments from the mint."

"What gives him that idea? I've heard crazy talk about robbing the Bank of California, but not a Wells Fargo shipment. Those shipments are guarded by U.S. Marshals, Sam. That's just more crazy talk." Donahue took a long pull on his hot brandy, lit a strong black cigar, and smiled at the diminutive clerk. Then he reconsidered... *Or is it crazy talk? It certainly wouldn't be the first shipment to be heisted.* Donahue listened carefully.

Owens spent the next hour explaining how Jaeckes had told him that he would pay him well if he would keep him advised of shipment dates and times, and how the duke had made the same proposal to Corcoran. By the time he was finished, the two had polished off two more large mugs of coffee and brandy and Donahue was giving the impression that he was now a believer.

The storm was making itself well known, destroying hanging signage, blowing down fences, creating massive snowdrifts, and clogging all the streets of the vibrant mining town. Donahue hadn't had a single customer except Sam Owens all morning until Tin Cup Duffy made his way in, bringing about twenty pounds of ice and snow with him.

"Damn, Michael, but if this keeps up, it might just get nasty out there. Hello Sam, how are you this fine morning?"

"Hello, Tin Cup," Sam said. The two rarely got past this stage in conversation. Tin Cup was loud and boisterous while Owens was quiet and reserved. There was no offer made but Tin Cup took it upon himself to join the table.

"Hot brandy?" he asked. "Oh, Michael, fill my little tin cup with some of that, please. You've a nice fire going. They can't even get the Old Corner Saloon open this morning. A tree fell right into the main door, and everything's jammed up."

"You'll only get one cup this morning, Duffy,"

Donahue said. "This storm will keep me more than busy around here, and I'll not have time to entertain the likes of you."

"One will be sufficient, Michael," Tin Cup said. He frowned, wanting to say more, but knew if he did, he'd be asked to leave. "Seen Terrence Corcoran this morning?"

"Probably won't see him much before this afternoon. Locatelli has him on the late shift again. Word came down the street yesterday that you were seen talking with that so-called European duke again. What would you and he have in common, Tin Cup? And why are you asking about Corcoran?"

Donahue was prodding the man, hoping that he would get angry and spout off something that could be passed to Corcoran. Tin Cup was one of those personalities who responded, that reacted without thinking, and that Donahue enjoyed prodding.

Owens got a little nervous, hearing Donahue bait Duffy that way. He stood up as if to leave and Donahue said, "No, Sam, sit for a while. I think we might have much to talk about."

"You have no reason to talk to me that way, Michael," Tin Cup whined. "Mr. Jaeckes has me in his employ now, and it's my responsibility to report to him often. Yesterday, I had much to tell him, as a matter of fact." He sat up straight, set his shoulders, and tried to look imperial.

"What kind of employment, Tin Cup Duffy? Cleaning the bathrooms?" Donahue laughed and even Sam Owens got a smile out of the comment. "Jaeckes is a phony, Duffy, and if you're doing anything for him, I'm sure it will lead to something illegal."

"His father is a member of the Royal Hungarian Family," Tin Cup snapped. "I've been engaged in keeping Mr. Jaeckes apprised of what's going on in town. He's very interested in Virginia City, in the mines, and in the people. I report to him regularly."

I bet you do, Donahue thought. *Finding out how the pay is distributed, when the shipments are due, and who might be available to help bring off the job. I won't say anymore so I don't arouse suspicions, but I'll certainly see to it that Terrence knows about all this.*

"I'm sure a man of your standing is a necessary part of a duke's retinue," Donahue chuckled. Tin Cup just looked at him, drank down the last of his hot brandy and made his way back into the maelstrom flailing about outside.

IT WAS VERY close to one o'clock that a mighty gust of wind blew the door of Locatelli's shack wide open, covering the sleeping Chief Deputy Terrence Corcoran in a blanket of icy snow. "Holy crap," he said, as he jumped from his bedroll and fought to get the door closed and jammed shut. He was in his long johns and barefoot, dancing about in cold snow, trying to wake up, cussing a blue streak.

Within half an hour, he had a roaring fire in the stove, clothing on, boots pulled on, and had a sense of the day. "I'm so hungry I could eat a whole buffalo," he said, stirring a pan full of side meat. He was looking around the shack, shaking his head some, and listening to the screaming winds outside. "I've got to do better than this," he murmured.

He sat on the edge of the cot. "Tomorrow's Christmas," he murmured. "Last Christmas I was in Elko working to save a herd of cattle stranded by a blizzard, now I'm in Virginia City about to be stranded by a blizzard." He was laughing as he sliced a potato up and threw it in with the bacon chunks, added chopped up onion, and looked around.

The walls were simple board and batten, allowing gusts of wind to whip right on through. The ceiling, he noticed was simply the bottom of the roofing boards, and snow drifted down from them as well.

The floor was rough boards, and the place was filled with things that Emilio Locatelli hadn't found time to take to the dump. "At a wage of two dollars a day, I can do a bit better than this," Corcoran snarled. "Maybe not a suite at the International," he chuckled, "but something with solid walls." He ate his breakfast right out of the pan, figuring it would freeze if he took the time to dish it onto a plate.

"It's a good thing the sun's up cuz I sure couldn't keep a candle burning in this wind." There was a shredded piece of cloth hanging near the window that may have been a curtain at one time, and it was blowing about like a witch's skirt. "Too cold to hang around here," he said, gulping down some almost boiling coffee.

Locatelli's place was on F Street, just one block up the hill from Chinatown. With the storms howling down the mountain, Corcoran didn't even bother trying to saddle old Rube. It was a miserable journey up Union Street two blocks, across the Virginia and Truckee railroad tracks at the E Street complex, and finally up to C Street.

He found the town virtually snowed in and plowed his way up one more, steep hill-climb to the courthouse. He was surprised to find it was so late in the afternoon. *I must have been mighty tired to sleep through this storm.* Locatelli was sitting at his desk drinking coffee and smoking a foul cigar.

"Mornin' boss," Terrence said. "I've missed these kinds of winter storms."

"Everybody in town has their wood stoves red hot, Terrence. One spark goes the wrong way, and up goes the town. Again. Bothers the hell out of me."

"Fireboys'll take care of it. Storm like this, there's so much snow, the fire wouldn't have a chance."

"Town burned to the ground once, Corcoran, it can happen again. Glad you're here. I'm goin' home. Town's all yours. Keep it safe. Good bye." He got up, threw on a massive bearskin coat, pulled on heavy gloves, and waddled out of the office. Corcoran poured a mug of coffee, searched around the sheriff's desk, found the flask, and added a bit of taste.

"I'll take a tour in an hour or so, then huddle up at the Silver Dollar Café for a steak about this big," he murmured. "A nice conversation with that lovely Suzanna O'Meara will make for a nice evening."

He was about to pour a third cup of coffee when Chester Fleming stormed into the office. "Better get down to the Washoe Club, Terrence. Boyington is tearing the joint up. Think he tried to cheat somebody again."

"Damn fool," Corcoran said. He pulled on the heavy

buffalo robe coat and followed Fleming out the door. It took a good fifteen minutes to make the three-block walk to the saloon. Snow was drifted in places as high as a man stood, and the wind came in hurricane gusts. "It's Christmas, Chester. He doesn't have the right to create problems on Christmas. How dare he," Corcoran laughed and snarled at the same time.

"It's a fine night for a fool. It's a fine night for me to shoot someone." Corcoran snarled, spit, growled, then chuckled fighting his way down Taylor Street and turned south to the Washoe Club. Taylor Street, between B and C Streets is very steep and he lost his footing, fell in a heap and slithered the last fifteen feet or so onto C Street.

"Maybe I'll shoot somebody twice." He cleared as much snow as possible, and got up onto the boardwalk in front of the Bank of California. The walkway was covered from the bank to the Washoe Club and Corcoran marched down the planks and pushed through the heavy double doors and into a melee.

Tables were turned over, chairs were broken, men were swinging fists and clubs, and Corcoran saw the flash of at least one knife. He pulled that big forty-five and put two slugs into the ceiling, bringing the action to a throbbing, calm. "I made up my mind I was going to shoot someone as I fought my way down here, boys. Who'll it be?"

"Better talk to Clarence Boyington before you shoot anyone, Terrence," Jeb Miner said. Half a dozen others chimed in in agreement.

"All right, you sleazy example of a gambler, what have you done now?" Corcoran walked over to one of the poker tables still standing. "Your days of being allowed to run a table in this town are numbered, Boyington. I've a mind to lift your license right now."

Boyington had a split lip and bloody nose, one eye was puffed up and turning purple and Corcoran was about to spin him around and put a set of handcuffs on the man when Boyington pulled a little pepper-box popper from his coat sleeve. A gambler's trick getting more and more popular.

"Back off, Corcoran. Everybody, stand back or die." He slowly edged around the gaming table and made his way toward the front doors. Angry men slowly gave way allowing him access to the doors.

Corcoran watched the man carefully, waiting for an opportunity to grab his weapon. Boyington never took his eyes off the deputy and everyone in the saloon knew that Corcoran would die if anyone made a move. There was just enough separation that Corcoran knew he couldn't make his move.

One man tripped. Boyington turned at the noise and Corcoran leaped at the man but Boyington saw him in time, fired, turned and ran hard out the doors. Corcoran staggered just a step and was right behind him.

Despite the heavy snow, wild winds, and icy cold, Boyington slammed through the heavy doors and into the night. Corcoran drew his weapon and barged through the crowd and out the doors. The storm had not let up at all, and Corcoran tried to find prints that Boyington might have left. He saw that the gambler had moved off the boardwalk and onto C Street, but the drifting snow covered every trace of the man from that point. All he could tell was that the man was headed toward where horses were tethered.

"I simply couldn't tell if he went north, south, east, or west after that" he later told the men in the saloon. "Was anyone hurt in the damn stupid fight that was going on?" He looked over at Jeb Miner.

"Did that shot hit you, Terrence? I saw you wince."

Corcoran pulled out of his heavy buffalo robe coat and when he handed it to Jeb Miner, a small lead ball fell to the floor. "Would you look at that!" Corcoran laughed. "Best coat I've ever had." He looked around at the chaos that was the Washoe Club prior to the night's activities.

"What the hell happened?"

"I'll tell you what happened," one of the men piped up. "He dealt me two nines which I held and asked for three cards. I filled out nines over aces and bet good on them. When I called him, that double-dealing fool showed me four aces. I whacked him across the head so hard he flew right out of his chair.

"I don't know what happened after that," the man said. "Somebody whacked me, and took all the money from the table."

"That's about the way it went, Terrence," Jeb Miner said.

"Well if that ain't all," Corcoran said. "We got us three or more crimes all at the same time, happenin' in the middle of the dangdest storm whatever. A card cheat, a thief what took the table money, and an assault with a deadly weapon on an officer of the law. I think I'll track old Boyington down when this storm lets up and just shoot the fool," he snarled angrily, adding,

"Somebody pour me a good shot of fine bourbon, if you will. I have another announcement to make."

He hiked himself up so he was sitting on the bar looking over the sea of faces. "I'm put up in a shack out behind Locatelli's place and it's a garbage dump. I need a home, cheap. Who's got a room for a fine upstanding young officer of the law?"

It was quiet. "Anyone?"

"I'll put you up, Corcoran," Jeb Miner said. "Two dollars a week and you'll have your own room and kitchen privileges. No women."

"My work here is done," Corcoran smiled.

He jumped down from the bar, clapped old Miner on the shoulder and headed toward the doors. "I'll be moving in soon's this storm gets through with its business, Mr. Miner, and thankee."

That was easy. What am I gonna do about Mr. Boyington? It would not be good for my reputation to allow that man to walk around these diggin's telling people he got away with pulling a gun on me. Guess I'll just shoot the bastard.

CHAPTER 7

It took a massive effort to make the journey from the Washoe Club north to the Silver Dollar Hotel for the steak dinner, but Corcoran, now with a new home to call his own, made it with only one stop.

"Michael, me lad, I see this raving tempest hasn't closed you down. I'm issuing a warrant for the arrest of Clarence Boyington, Mr. Donahue, so if you should happen to run into the foul man, let me know, please. Or, just shoot him."

"Our gambling friend has done you wrong?"

"Pulled a gun on me, he did. He pulled the trigger but the bullet couldn't penetrate this fine buffalo robe coat I'll never ever give up. I don't much appreciate a man pulling a gun on me."

Donahue had to chuckle over that, knowing that Corcoran would pull his own gun at the slightest provocation. Corcoran spent the next ten minutes discussing the ruckus at the Washoe Club. "Man's a fool, Michael. Oh, I do have some good news, though. I'll be renting a room from Jeb Miner. Mr. Corcoran is moving uptown, sir. Anything going on around town I should know about?"

"Not much chance of skullduggery, Terrence. Not in this maelstrom. Sam Owens stopped by this morning and told me what Jaeckes wants. Are you in favor of this? Also, it appears that Tin Cup is now working for Jaeckes. Slippery man with a syrup covered tongue, that so-called duke is."

"I plan to pass on to the U.S. Marshals down at the mint anything that Owens passes on to Jaeckes and anything that velvet-wearing duke should tell him. If there is a plot, the marshals will end it quickly" He shook his head to an offer of coffee and brandy and headed for the door.

"I didn't get much to eat yesterday, Michael. And only some half-frozen bacon when I woke up today. I can almost taste a steak this thick waiting for me at the Silver Dollar. I'll be back later."

It was a grueling two long blocks through heavy snowdrifts and the long stairway down to the restaurant at the hotel. If he passed someone on the journey he didn't notice. Every business on the east side of C Street was closed. He couldn't see the west side the snow drifts were so deep.

I'd bet even the railroad can't get through in a blizzard like this, and I'm sure none of the teamsters are moving about. I might have to put together a group of men to do some house checking, make sure everyone is okay. It's in a storm like this that those boys working underground are the most comfortable. He chortled thinking about that.

"Ah, lovely Miss O'Meara," he said, shedding that buffalo robe coat and its accumulated ten pounds of ice and snow. He hung his floppy sombrero with a little flourish, smiling at the lady. "I would have been here earlier, but had to take care of a bit of a ruckus downtown. With this storm, are you serving supper?"

"It's nice to see you again, Mr. Corcoran. Coffee to start?" He nodded and took a seat so that he could see most of the rest of the tables in the small restaurant. He was the only customer. Mostly, he could watch Suzanna walk around and through the restaurant.

"What would you like with that hot coffee? We have beef steaks and roast lamb from the Carson Valley, roast pork from the Truckee Meadows, and roast venison from Nevada's wilderness," she laughed.

"I had a thick steak in mind," he said. "On the other hand, I could eat an entire roast shoulder of pork. Lots of potatoes, and gallons of gravy, if you please." He offered another generous smile with the order. She scurried into the kitchen and he could hear her putting his order together.

When she brought it out, a platter filled with sliced pork, heaps of mashed potatoes, all covered in deep brown gravy, a basket filled with hot biscuits, and a tub of cooled butter. "Oh, my," he said. "This will keep my blood from freezing."

He noticed that besides no customers, only he and Suzanna were in the restaurant. There was no one in the kitchen. *This lovely lass fought the storm and is running this café all by herself. I hope she gives the rest of the employees the devil for not showing up.*

"Won't you join me, Miss O'Meara?" She hesitated for just a moment, and sat down opposite the deputy. "Have you had any dealings with this Elon Jaeckes?" He figured that if Tin Cup was really working for the man, he might have talked about Jaeckes with Suzanna.

"He's a very rude man," she said, quickly. "I wish Tin Cup wasn't working for him. He wants people to believe that he's Hungarian, but to me," and her face carried a definite scowl, "he's a scoundrel of the first order. Tin Cup insists the man will make him rich, and soon. I've warned Mr. Duffy several times that the man is up to something illegal.

"I've travelled in Europe, Mr. Corcoran, met royalty, and this man is scum. Everything is affected, not natural. His carriage is not royalty, it's something he thinks is royalty. The man is a fake. Even his accent is fake, Mr. Corcoran." She seemed incensed over the mere thought of the man, and Corcoran was glad he'd brought up the subject.

"I have those same feelings," Corcoran said. "How strong is the connection between Tin Cup and Jaeckes?" *This is more than I hoped for. Suzanna is apparently an astute and well-educated young lady. I wonder just how close she is to Duffy? She gives me the impression that she would be smarter than to get too close.*

"I've begged Mr. Duffy to stay away from the man, but he's not willing to see how he's being used. Jaeckes gives him a ten-dollar gold piece from time to time and Tin Cup thinks he's doing well."

"What does he actually do for the man?" Corcoran felt he was getting close but didn't want to press too much. "Jaeckes, through Duffy also asked me to gather information for him, but I told him I already had a fine job."

"According to Tin Cup, he and several other men are

asked to deliver information. Now that's not a crime, Mr. Corcoran, but when I asked him what kind of information, Tin Cup hedged some. I stiffened my shoulders, Mr. Corcoran, and asked in a good Irish way, just what kind of information, Mr. Duffy?"

Corcoran chuckled, seeing her doing that, hearing the ring of County Cork in her voice, and feeling the rap of strong Irish knuckles on the back of his hand. *I'm hearing me own mother talking here. It's like a choir of angels singing to hear a lady talk like that.* "Did he straighten up and stand tall as my own mother might say?"

"He did not, sir." Suzanna got up and brought the coffee pot over, poured more for each of them and sat back down. "I've talked with others, though, who believe that Jaeckes is trying to get information about various deliveries of money to the bank. I'm sure he's planning to rob the bank."

"That bank is as safe as any bank I've ever seen. He would have to be stupid to give it a try. If he does, and if Tin Cup is involved, you know I'll have to arrest them. I hope you understand it's my job."

"I would want you to, Mr. Corcoran. I would demand it. Tin Cup and I do not have the relationship he tried to get you to believe, sir. If he becomes a criminal, you must arrest him."

I'd rather just shoot the fool. I like what I just heard, though. "I will do that, Miss O'Meara. I will. On another note, I have found living quarters. The sheriff had me set up in a shack in his back yard, but I've found a nice apartment at Jeb Miner's."

"I like Mr. Miner. He's a true gentleman, as are you, Mr. Corcoran. I live just two doors from Mr. Miner. It's not as noisy as some of the other areas." She smiled remembering when she'd lived closer to one of the major mines.

The mines were all located right in town, of course. It was the city that grew up around the mines. Blasting took place all day and all night. The great Cornish steam pumps operated around the clock, pumping hot water from the deep mines. Virginia City sat on top of an active geothermal system and the mines dug right into it.

Adolph Sutro drove his tunnel in from the Dayton Valley to drain the mines, but by the time he reached the mines, at 1,750 feet underground, the mines were already hundreds of feet below that. Mills pulverized the ore with heavy stamps, great steam engines drove hundreds of hoist operations, drove saws to cut timber, and there were the usual sounds of more than a hundred saloons filled with men coming off shift or those getting ready to go on shift.

"Virginia City can be a noisy place to live," she chuckled, giving Corcoran a big smile. "I made apple pie. Would you like a slice and more coffee?" His smile said yes and their conversation continued for another half hour or more.

The storm was raging and Terrence Corcoran finally knew he had to get to work. "I must get back out on the street, dear lady. Trouble is always waiting its chance to strike. Will you be okay here, alone?"

"I'll be fine, Terrence. I was planning to keep the café open all night." He perked up, understanding that this was the first time she had called him Terrence, and he wondered if he dared to call her Suzanna?

"I'll check back with you later, Miss O'Meara," he smiled. "If you need someone to walk you home in the morning, I'll be available and at your service."

"I believe we are now friends, and so, I would be pleased if you would call me Suzanna." His smile would have been seen clear to the bottom of Six Mile Canyon if it weren't for the storm. She continued, "I would like to be escorted home, Terrence." He wanted to do a little dance as he took the long stairway from the café back up to C Street and the waiting blizzard.

CORCORAN FLOUNDERED his way up to the courthouse and a warm office. "So Tin Cup and several others are feeding information from the bank and Wells Fargo to our little velvet covered duke," he murmured, tossing some big chunks of oak into his wood stove. "I need to know the other names. Who else is feeding information? Bank clerks? More than Sam Owens at Wells Fargo?"

He remembered Claire telling him about Lathrop, Smithson, and Boyington. "Well then," he murmured. "I've already shot Lathrop, so just Smithson and Boyington to go. Boyington is a card sharp, she called him a thief, and now, he's wanted for taking a shot at me. Yup, gotta shoot that man."

He wrote up what happened at the Washoe Club so the sheriff would be aware when he arrived and he had questions for the sheriff, as well. *I've been carrying this old tin badge for two days now and know about a possible gang of outlaws planning to rob the Bank of California and possibly a gold shipment from the mint and old man Locatelli hasn't mentioned either one. Oh, and the new D.A. Mr. Ezra McNabb warned me off getting in Jaeckes' face. How do you spell conspiracy?*

Corcoran was chuckling to himself as he wrestled back into the buffalo robe coat and headed out to the snow-packed streets of Virginia City, He found no tracks along B Street and turned down Taylor Street to C where tracks also didn't exist. "Those guys underground are as comfortable as if they were in the Sandwich Islands and up here, a man could die fast."

It was one of the problems that the hard-rockers faced working the Comstock deep mines. Ten hours underground in high temperature and high humidity, and then coming to the surface and into minus temperatures, ice, and snow, and the moisture in the lungs condensed to liquid. Instant pneumonia. Many suffered from consumption, and were known to be troubled with the cons.

Corcoran took a tour through what was known as the Barbary Coast, a rough and dangerous part of town, slipped down to D Street and fought his way back up north, and at Mill Street, returned to C Street. The walk would normally take less than half an hour. Tonight, it was a two-hour adventure. There was a layer of ice under the snow and Corcoran went down more than twice. The language following each mishap was ferocious.

He found Michael Donahue's Sazerac open, and fought his way into the warmth. "All the saints in heaven have left, Michael, and it's the devil's doing that's driving this storm. Would you have a wee taste of hot brandy back there?" He fought clear of the heavy coat and walked to a table. "I think I'll sit a spell, sir. I think some of the drifts are more than four feet now, and there's no let-up in this storm at all."

"Has anyone talked to you about Daniel McKenzie?" Michael asked, bringing a steaming cup of coffee well laced with brandy to the table.

"I remember a McKenzie, Michael. Wasn't he the head of the Miner's Union or something?"

"That's the man. Seems they've been checking the books and he may have slipped several thousand dollars into his own poke. Might want to ask Locatelli about that."

"I'm worrying about this sheriff I've come home to. He's not mentioned a word about a possible gang looking to rob the bank or hold up a gold shipment. Now you tell me about a theft of the Miner's Union, and it's the first I've heard of that.

"I think Mr. Locatelli and I need to have a long discussion, and I'm afraid I might just have to shoot the man again."

There was little humor in the comment, Michael Donahue noticed. "Did McKenzie leave town?"

"Some believe so, others aren't so sure. Don't know why he'd stay, though."

CHAPTER 8

"It was the most miserable of nights and the most wonderful," Corcoran said to Donald Ferguson when the clerk arrived at the courthouse. "I had supper with a charming lady and was able to escort her home, which made my heart feel good."

"Well, good for you, Terrence. I see this storm is starting to let up a little bit."

"Aye 'tis, and it made my job immensely difficult, but that wasn't the worst of it. Clarence Boyington threw a fit again, but worse, pulled a weapon and shot at me as I was breaking up the Donnybrook. I've issued a call for his arrest but if you could get the D.A. to issue a warrant, I would appreciate it. There's a lack of respect for the law in this old town, Mr. Ferguson," Corcoran said, that wry smile spreading across his rough face.

"I have no idea when Locatelli might make it in this morning, but my twelve hours were up a couple of hours ago."

"Before you leave, I'd like to have a private word

with you, Terrence. If the sheriff isn't here yet, maybe we could step into his office for a moment."

Corcoran was surprised by Ferguson's request, but nodded, and they walked across the courthouse to the sheriff's office. Corcoran had the potbelly stove almost red hot and the coffee was boiling away. He poured them each a cup and found the sheriff's little flask, poured some himself and Ferguson said no.

"So, my fine friend, is something bothering you?" Corcoran sat in the sheriff's chair and Ferguson remained standing, almost pacing, in deep thought. "Are you in some kind of trouble?"

"I feel I can trust you, Terrence, that you're an honest man. What I'm about to tell you must be kept in absolute confidence. If not, if something is said, it will cause my death and probably yours as well."

"My goodness, Donald, are you in that deep of trouble? Of course, you can trust me, and if you need help, you've come to the right man." *Here comes that thought from late last night. Yes, Donald Ferguson, I can spell conspiracy. He knows something; it has to do with the district attorney, and it could get him killed. This old town has changed in the couple of years I was gone.*

"Whatever it is Donald, first, know that you can trust me, and if you're in trouble, know too that I'm a friend. Just be careful who you talk to and what you say."

Ferguson quit pacing, decided to fill his cup after all, and sat down, looking more serious than Corcoran had ever seen him. He was wearing a well-cut wool suit, starched collar, wool vest, and string tie. He reached inside his suit coat to an inside pocket and brought out a finely tooled leather wallet, flipped it open and laid it on the desk in front of Corcoran.

"My God in heaven," Terrence said staring at the very shiny shield that announced in no uncertain terms, Special Agent, Well Fargo Security. "Maybe we shouldn't talk about this right now, Donald. The walls in this courthouse have many ears, and Locatelli is due in at any moment."

"You've worked in this blizzard all night and I know you're tired. Go home and sleep. I leave the office at four. Let's meet at the Corner Saloon at Piper's Opera House when I get off. There are private tables where we can't be heard or seen." Ferguson tucked his credentials back in his suit jacket, nodded with a generous smile to the deputy, and slipped back into the district attorney's office.

"The surprises of this day are endless," Corcoran chuckled. "Were I a betting man, and of course I am, I would say that Mr. McNabb and Mr. Jaeckes are under investigation by Wells Fargo. I'm betting that Mr. Locatelli is also on that man's list." He was mumbling and jumped when the sheriff stormed into the office.

"Damn this storm," Locatelli said. He squirmed out of a heavy full fur parka, probably bearskin, and offered both hands to the potbelly stove. "Who were you talking to?"

"Myself," Corcoran chuckled. "I'm a good listener. Glad you're here cuz I'm out of here. Report's on the desk." He found his buffalo robe coat and headed out the door. *Thank all the gods of ancient Greece that Ferguson*

and I were not in deep conversation. There are those times
when things do seem to fall into place without causing chaos.

CORCORAN FOUND his way to the shack, busting through
drifts that reached his waist and more, fell down more
times than he could count on the treacherously steep
hill, and didn't even take his clothes off when he fell
onto the cot and pulled wool blankets over his head.
Goodbye cruel world.

Dreams of Suzanna O'Meara got mixed up with
visions of Wells Fargo Security Agents and Hungarian
dukes in royal velvet. Always lingering somewhere in
the dream was a vision of Claire Donnegan, dancing,
flirting, and dead.

Serious banging on the shack door brought the
deputy awake. He had his Colt in hand when he pulled
the door open. "Sorry to bother you, Terrence, but it's
important."

"Sam Owens. My God man, come in. Let me get the
stove hot. What time is it?" Corcoran wasn't even close
to awake, put the weapon back in its holster and stirred
hot coals around before slipping some kindling into the
stove. "Looks like the storm's gone off to Utah or
somewhere."

"Clear and icy cold right now. It's about three
o'clock, Terrence." Owens had a worried look on his
face, slipped out of his coat and sat down on the edge of
the cot. "This isn't the nicest place to live," he said.
There was a look of dismay on the man's face as he
looked through cracks in the walls to the bright

outdoors, and other cracks in the ceiling, dripping melted snow onto the interior.

"I'm moving up to Jeb Miner's place later today. Rented a room from him. So, Mr. Owens, what brings you down here? You look like you're worried about something."

"Mr. Jaeckes wants me to tell him when the next shipment of gold coins is arriving from the mint. He offered me five hundred dollars for the information."

"We were expecting something like that," Corcoran said. *Five hundred dollars is considerable money, but a shipment of gold and silver coin is measured in six figures, so those three aren't that much. Our first crime has been committed.*

"I wasn't, but there's more," the small chief clerk said. "If I don't tell him and the shipment arrives, he threatened to kill me. That monster servant of his smiled when he said that, and flourished a huge sword."

"The Marshal Service will have to be told, Owens. I'll send a wire."

"I told the sheriff and he scoffed at the comments. Told me I was imagining things. Suggested I didn't hear the man right. Maybe his accent, the sheriff said. He simply didn't believe me, Terrence."

"The sheriff hasn't been feeling well," Corcoran smiled. "Let's keep this information just between us, your bosses, and the marshals, shall we? Based on what the Marshal Service has to say, it'll just be you and me working together." Owens nodded, trying to smile.

The word conspiracy flowed through the deputy's mind, visions of that Wells Fargo security shield could be seen, and Corcoran poured coffee for the two of them. "Don't mention this to anyone else, Sam. There's more going on than either one of us knows right now. I'll alert the mint, and I may have help coming my way.

"We expected this, but the threats change the picture. Who else was there when you had this conversation?" Maybe he could get some names of others who worked for the duke. Other than Tin Cup and the black giant.

"Just Tin Cup and Clarence Boyington," he said. "As I was leaving, Orin Lathrop came in. Did you know they cut off his arm? Right above the elbow."

"Yeah, I heard. I shot him a few days ago." *Maybe that's why he was waiting for me down Six Mile. I did tell a few people I was coming back to Virginia town. But even so, it still doesn't make any sense.*

"Okay, Sam, you head back to your office and notify the right people at Wells Fargo and I'll let the marshals know what's going on, and I'll do everything I can to protect you. Let's not talk about this with anyone, in particular, the sheriff or DA."

Owens pulled himself into his heavy coat and headed out into a frozen world of wind and ice. Corcoran shaved and swilled coffee, and headed up to the sheriff's office and his turn at protecting the good souls of Virginia City. *What the heck have I come home to? If McNabb and Locatelli are involved in this heist, who got it started? Jaeckes is a con man from the word go. He is not a European duke, he's a city slicker criminal. I don't know anything about this McNabb feller, and maybe need to find out a whole lot.*

"SORRY I'M LATE, Donald. We've got ourselves a nest full of criminals, I'm afraid." He made the long trek up the steep roadway to Piper's Opera House and the Corner Saloon. "I'm going to let you talk first and then I'll fill you in on what I've learned in just two or three days. It was below zero when I left the shack and with night coming on, it's gonna be a miserable shift, el friendo."

"You might remember, Terrence, that I arrived in Virginia City about a week before you shot the sheriff and had to leave town. Wells Fargo had heard rumors of a major operation to take place here, and sent me up. McNabb arrived two weeks later followed by his nibs, Jaeckes. It's taken them this long to put an organization together, but I believe the next coin shipment from Carson City will be hit."

"It's amazing just to consider. Those shipments are still coming by wagon? Why not the railroad? Hell, Sharon is the bank manager and partner in the railroad. That would be the logical means of transportation. Wells Fargo has the contract to move the coins and has special rail cars for just that. What am I missing?" Terrence Corcoran sat back in his chair and sipped on his coffee, giving Ferguson time to put answers together.

"You're right on everything except one thing. The shipment is sent by rail, Terrence. But it still has to be unloaded into wagons to be brought from the freight depot up to the bank. That's where things are going to go wrong. All those crates of twenty-dollar gold pieces have to be unloaded and loaded at the depot, then unloaded and taken into the bank on C Street.

"Big opportunities for problems, according to the

bank and of course, Wells Fargo. During the exchange at the rail yard is the most vulnerable time, but what comes to mind, Corcoran, what the hell do you do with tons of coins?" Ferguson laughed, seeing all those coins in huge crates that simply can't be tucked into a saddle bag by the crook as he rides off into a blazing horizon.

"Wait until the crates are loaded onto the wagons and then hit them," Corcoran smiled.

"Yes, but we're talking three wagons." Ferguson just shook his head. "What do you do, simply drive those heavy wagons off somewhere?"

"Somebody has their head on backwards," Corcoran said with a sly smile. "Jaeckes had a talk with Sam Owens, demanding that he be notified of the next shipment's date and times. Threatened the little guy's life if he didn't do it. I sent that information to the marshals at the mint and told Sam to notify Wells Fargo. Jaeckes is relying on people like Tin Cup Duffy and Orin Lathrop, and that's about as stupid as you can get. Neither man wears shoes because they can't tie the laces."

Ferguson almost spit coffee out his nose at that comment and had a coughing session that lasted a full minute. "My people tell me that McNabb, as we know him, is actually from Chicago by way of New Orleans, and known there as Johnny Carlisle, a con-man, murderer, rapist, and bank robber. An all-around nice guy."

"Is he really an attorney? He gets himself all puffed up like one, but does he have training or been made an attorney? He tried to boss me, tried to tell me how to do my job, and that's not what district attorneys do.

"He's definitely proud of himself," Corcoran continued. "Where does Locatelli come into the picture? He's been pretty straight since I've known him. He doesn't much care for bad guys."

"I think he's on the outside fringe at best. Maybe fed wrong information and swallows it. He can't see past what he's told, you know."

"I do know that. The man has no creative spirit. So, McNabb slash Carlisle is the honcho, Jaeckes is made to look like the front guy, and Locatelli is told that Jaeckes is really a Hungarian duke and all is okay. Is that the picture?"

"Pretty much. Orrin Lathrop is rounding up gunmen, Boyington is working with him, and your friend and mine, Tin Cup Duffy is hired to do whatever needs to be done. The riff-raff of the Comstock is primed to commit the biggest robbery in history." He was chuckling, still snorting coffee, and punched the tabletop a couple of times. "What are we gonna do about all this, Terrence Corcoran?"

They were laughing at the picture Ferguson had drawn and at first simply wanted to file the information away. "If it weren't for the threats, I'd say all of this is simply a big joke. Tin Cup, Lathrop, and Boyington involved in a heist of this size would be a good stage show comedy if it weren't for the death threats." Corcoran sat back in his chair, had a sip of cold beer.

"If the gold comes here on the train, it has to be moved from the depot to the bank. And if McNabb has a small army of gunslingers pulling it off, it has to be taken somewhere. Stay with me, Ferguson," Corcoran chuckled. "Those wagon loads of booty weigh tons and take up lots of space. Whoever put this plan together is an idiot and it's going to cost lives."

Corcoran was about to say something when a man ran into the Corner Saloon screaming his name. "I'm right here, old man. What's the problem?" Corcoran was on his feet immediately, found his hand curling around the handle of that big revolver, and ready for a fight.

"Come quick, Terrence. It's Claire Donnegan."

"Claire? What, Johnson? What's happened to Claire?"

"She's dead," he said.

"Oh, my God, what happened?" Corcoran was slipping into his heavy buffalo robe coat. Skipper Johnson usually saw to it that the ladies of the night were kept safe from fools and troublemakers, and Corcoran could see the hurt in the man's eyes.

"She was murdered, Terrence. I checked on her just an hour or so ago and when I checked just now, I found her on her bed with her throat slashed. Oh, God, Terrence, this is terrible."

"Tell me what you saw as we walk down to her crib, Skipper. Was she dressed? Was the place ransacked? Could you tell if she fought back? Just start talking as we make our way through the leftovers of this maniacal storm."

All thoughts of a heist of gold and silver coins left his mind, he left Donald Ferguson sitting at the table, and could only think of Claire Donnegan and who might have killed the woman.

"You said she was alive just a few hours ago?" Johnson nodded. "Did you see anyone around the place?

This isn't normally a busy time for the working girls." Johnson indicated again that he hadn't seen or heard anything before stumbling onto the horrible scene.

"All right, then, go get the undertaker while I see if I can figure out what happened. We'll talk some more after we get this cleaned up." Johnson hurried back out into the bitter cold.

CHAPTER 9

It's all right there in the report, Sheriff," Corcoran said as Sheriff Locatelli arrived at the office. "Sorry for getting you up, but I thought you would want to know about this." Corcoran sent Skipper Johnson to get the sheriff after he made his preliminary investigation and had Johnson write up his statement as well. The undertaker took Claire's sundered body away to make her ready for burial.

"It was an ugly murder. That gal fought back hard. Whoever did this will have some serious scratches, probably on his neck and face. There were gobs of skin and blood under Claire's fingernails. The bastard made some ugly slashes with his knife and then pretty much tore the place apart. As if he was looking for something."

"You keep saying he, Terrence. Are you sure it's a man we will be looking for? You know how these doves are always getting into fights." The sheriff had his heavy coat hung up and a cup of coffee in hand when he sat behind his desk. He was reading Corcoran's report first.

"Must have been a lot of blood. Any traces of that or footprints outside the crib? Or inside?"

"Yeah, that's why I keep saying he. Big bloody footprints inside, and I followed a set outside until they got all jumbled up with others. The man left the crib, ran north on D Street, then turned up to C. That's where I lost his trail. Looked like he turned north on C Street, but too many other footprints covered his.

"Whoever it was, is a big man. The prints from his boots are larger than mine, even larger that Skipper Johnson's. With this storm, he was on foot. Riding a horse or driving a team is simply out of the question."

Corcoran walked to the stove and stuck a chunk of oak in, grabbed the coffee pot and poured each of them a fresh cup. "Claire, like so many of the girls, spent her money as fast as she made it, but our killer gave her place a going over looking for something."

"Thanks for calling me out on this, Corcoran. Spread the word up and down the streets. With the storm, it's a good bet the killer is still in town. Let's see if we can wrap this up quickly. Anything other than boot prints to go on?"

"Boot prints and probable deep scratches, sheriff," Corcoran said. "Bloody clothing has been burned by now, I would think. If he did find some money, he'd surely be spending it. I'll stop at all the hotels, restaurants, and saloons, spread the word down to Gold Hill, Silver City, Dayton, and Johntown. We'll get him."

Corcoran was watching Locatelli read through the reports as he got back into his buffalo robe coat and headed into the below zero night. *Poor dear Claire. Little darlin', I'll find the foul person that did this and he'll pay and pay some more.* Corcoran carried a soft spot about a mile wide for the working girls of the mining camps. He could ride into any camp from the length of the Sierra Nevada, and from New Mexico to Wyoming, and be called by name along the bordello roads.

"I BETTER HAVE another hot brandy, Michael me lad," Corcoran said. "What do you make of all this? I stopped by the firehouse and the boys are in an uproar. They plan to tear the town apart until they find the monster that killed Claire Donnegan."

"They just might do that, Terrence," Donahue laughed. "She was their darlin', you know, an angel during their times of need," and he chuckled some. "You weren't here during that last flu epidemic, but those fire boys will tell you how Claire put together a brigade of soiled doves.

"They made great kettles of soup and stew, nursed and fed the firefighters, kept them warm and well, and you must believe, those fire laddies appreciated the effort. Yes, laddie buck, they might very well tear this old town to shreds to find her killer."

"I for one will welcome their help," Corcoran said. He finished his mug of hot coffee well laced with brandy and struggled into his great coat. "Let me know if you hear anything of if something strange should strike your fancy." He walked to the window and looked out on the frozen street scene.

"Isn't it supposed to be spring? It looks like some of the men from John Mackay's mines are trying to shovel the streets clear. Or he's planning to send the snow to the mill." Donahue was laughing hard as Corcoran had to force the door to get it open. "What a night," he said, and walked out into sub-arctic temperatures. The men with shovels were flinging the stuff toward the sidewalks and the Washoe zephyr was sending it right back at them.

Most of the businesses were closed, street lamps hadn't been lit, and only a few of the saloons were open. His first stop was the saloon in Mollinelli's Hotel. He noticed a light on inside the brewery across the street as he slipped through the heavy swinging doors. "Evenin', Emil. Got some bad news to pass along."

He spent several minutes telling Emil Rathburn about Claire's murder and made sure the elderly barman understood he wanted to catch the killer sooner, not later. "I see lamps lit over at the brewery. Making beer, are they?"

"Noticed that, too, Corcoran. Unusual." Rathburn spoke in two and three-word sentences, and few of them. He walked down the length of the bar toward windows that looked out on the main street. "Shadows moving."

Corcoran joined him and they watched shadows move across filthy windows inside the brewery. "I think I'll take a look-see." The deputy fought his way across the snow and ice on C Street and rapped on the brewery door. No one came to the door and he took his revolver out and gave the door a good solid couple of whacks. "Wake the dead and those fools can't hear me?"

It was the second hard pounding with the butt of his weapon that he finally heard someone walk up to the door. "We ain't open. Go away," a snarly voice said.

"It's Deputy Terrence Corcoran. Open up." He heard a second person come up to the door, but it still didn't open.

"Go away, Corcoran, we're busy in here."

"That you, Smithson? Damn it, it's cold out here. Open up."

"Not tonight, Corcoran. Go mind your business somewhere else. We're busy." Corcoran heard two people walk away from the door, and laughter from several others inside.

This is strange. Ike Smithson and several others are working on something that doesn't have anything to do with beer. I wonder who's in there with him? Sounded like at least three or four people laughing. He slipped over to the window and found that the lower half of the tall window had been blocked off from the inside. He could see that lamps were lit but that's all. Shadows fell across the upper half of the window, but they told him nothing.

He went back to the hotel and ordered a cup of coffee, sitting at the very end of the bar so he could watch the brewery. "They got a back door to that brewery, Emil?"

"Not from this level. There are large doors on the D Street level for wagons to back up for loading those barrels. What's going on?"

"Got me," Corcoran said, drinking his coffee. "I might sit a spell, Emil. Keep you company. Why are you even open?"

"Mines are still operating, Terrence. Miners still drink after shift." They chuckled at the thought. "That my law-dog friend is a great truth."

IT WAS a full hour later that Corcoran saw the lamps being doused but no one came out of the brewery. *They're going into the basement and will come out on D Street. I gotta get down there.*

It was hard trying to move fast through the drifted snow and ice clogging the streets, but he slip-slided his way down Union Street and turned north onto D Street. He was about fifty yards or so from the back of the brewery when he saw four men come out onto the loading dock. A large freight wagon with four-up was waiting for them, and he watched helplessly as they jumped into the wagon and the driver turned north. The teams were big and strong and had little trouble breaking their way through the drifts of snow and ice. They made their way north and Corcoran noticed they did not make the turn east on Mill Street.

Not two hours ago I told the sheriff that a murderer was probably still in town because a wagon just couldn't go anywhere. Damn me. They may not be going fast but they sure as all get out are going. Heading north, though. Where would they be going? If they had turned down Mill Street, they could have been heading for Butters' Mill or the Flowery, or even all the way to Sutro. But north?

He watched the wagon going north until it was out of sight. *They're heading for Lousetown. One of those men was Ike Smithson and I'm sure another was Tin Cup Duffy. What were they doing and why would they leave at this hour and drive to Lousetown?*

Lousetown was in the flats about five miles north of Virginia City and was host to a racetrack and several skin and bone ranches. "There isn't one valid reason for those men to be going north, bucking heavy snow drifts and chunks of ice, fighting temperatures to make a bear worry, and no open saloons." He had to chuckle at his own comment and turned back up to C Street.

"Mr. MINER, sir, or should I say, Mr. Landlord, sir," Corcoran said. "Looks like you're the few customers in any saloon in town." He worried the questions about Ike Smithson and the brewery all the way down the street to the Washoe Club. "It's a cold and quiet night out. The faro tables at the International Hotel are even empty."

"Terrence." Miner was nursing a mug of coffee that surely had a dollop or two of whiskey in it. "Is it true what I heard about Claire Donnegan? She was murdered?"

"I'm afraid so, Jeb. Nasty business. Used a knife and did terrible damage. Heard anything else?" Corcoran got yet another cup of coffee and grabbed a couple of cigars from the box on the bar. "The killer is a large man with big feet, and that's all I know."

"Boyington, Duffy, and a half dozen others I can think of have big feet," Jeb Miner said. "Is it a revenge killing? Or a fight among the girls?"

"I think the original motive might have been robbery, Jeb. The place was torn apart. I stumbled into something going on at the brewery. Smithson and several other men working on something. Wouldn't talk to me. Heard anything?"

"Yup. In fact, I was planning to try to find you later, Corcoran," Miner said. "You remember me telling you about this Elon Jaeckes and my thoughts of him looking to rob the Bank of California? I think he's got Smithson involved now, too. I don't know exactly doing what, but surely involved. If I were you, I'd wring Tin Cup's neck a bit."

"Lathrop, Duffy, Smithson, and many others seem to be involved, Jeb. What are your feelings about McNabb? He tried to tell me not to investigate our velvet wearing Hungarian duke."

"Did Locatelli back him up?"

"No, not at all. But I'm also worrying about our dear sheriff. What exactly have I come home to? I have a dreadful feeling that McNabb and Locatelli are involved with this Jaeckes fool and are after more than just robbing the bank. Half the rowdies in town almost sneer at me, thinking that they're safe. McNabb didn't even follow through on charges against Lathrop for trying to kill me.

"You and Michael Donahue are the only friends I have right now. As soon as these streets clear up, I'm going to take a ride to Carson City, get me some answers."

"If you take the train, Terrence, I'll go with you." He sat back in his chair and snickered a bit. "I still hurt too much to ride a horse all that distance. Doc Williams said I might not be able to go back to work. He said I should buy a bar and just sit and watch the barman do his work."

"Splendid idea, old man." Corcoran said. "I'll be honored to be known as one of your outstanding customers."

"About McNabb." Miner looked around at the

empty bar, making sure it was still empty. The barman was at the far end cleaning something and there were no dealers at any of the tables. "I've got the feeling that he came to town with a purpose, a plan, and that plan has nothing to do with being district attorney. That's just a ruse. There are huge amounts of money that move through this little town, bucko. He wants some of it."

"Would you be thinking gold and silver coins, or gold and silver bullion? Either way, the problem is weight," Corcoran said. Miner just nodded, a grin on his face, probably wondering which it would be, coin or bullion.

Corcoran made one more stop on his swing through Virginia City. "It's a cold one, Mr. Jackson."

"It is that, Corcoran," the faro dealer at the International Hotel said. "We've had three men come through our gaming parlor tonight, and not one stopped. At least the streets are slowly getting cleared.

"What a terrible shame about Claire Donnegan. Fire Chief O'Reilly is planning a massive parade when the streets are cleared, to take the dear girl to her final resting place. He said every piece of rolling stock of every fire brigade on the Comstock will be involved."

Like so many of the men who came to the Comstock when it became known just how rich the diggings would be, Jackson had a soft spot for the working girls. There were a few tents spread across the face of Mt. Davidson back in 1859, maybe fifty or so ragtag prospectors panning enough "color" to keep them interested. They threw away great clumps of heavy blue-black material that clogged their riffle boxes. Jackson remembered that stuff was as heavy as gold and really jammed the works.

They weren't hard rock miners, weren't mining engineers. It was years before someone had an assay done and that blue stuff turned out to be almost pure silver. From a few tents and coyote holes, Mt. Davidson's flanks soon had hold of one of the largest cities west of the Rocky Mountains, certainly the richest.

There was a legend at the time that one of the original locators, a man from Virginia who was known as Old Virginny, slipped and fell in a drunken walk home to his coyote hold one night and spilled some whiskey from his bottle. "I dub thee Virginia Town," he bellowed, and the town has been Virginia City since. Corcoran believed the tale as did many others.

Jackson was a young man who followed the cry, "On to Washoe," and made his way from the gold fields of California to this new bonanza. That was so many years ago, he remembered, and the man left the deep mines for the safety of a faro table. "Without those lovely ladies, Terrence, my early days here would have been dreadful indeed. You find that vile person that killed Claire. You find him and kill him, Terrence."

"I will, Jackson," Corcoran said. "Does this Mr. Jaeckes ever play at your table?"

"He understands the game rather well," the dealer said. A smile crept across his face as he thought about it. "I believe he's had quite a bit of experience bucking the table. Maybe even had a table of his own."

That was a revelation to Corcoran and caught the deputy by surprise. "A member of European royalty as a faro dealer? Surely, you're pulling a bit on my leg, Mr. Jackson."

"Not at all, Corcoran," Jackson said. "Jaeckes is an accomplished player, and I've noticed that his accent seems to leave him at times when the table bucks back." Jackson was chuckling remembering how he took several hundred dollars from the man a night or two ago.

Corcoran said goodnight and headed back up to B Street and the warmth of the sheriff's cubbyhole. *Our velvet-wearing duke is a faro dealer? Our splendidly dressed European royal doesn't always speak with a Hungarian accent? Yes, Terrence my man, we will be making that trip to Carson City as soon as the railroad gets moving. We may even try to validate the district attorney's credentials, eh?*

CHAPTER 10

"IT REALLY DOES FEEL LIKE SPRING, TERRENCE. JUST FOUR days ago we couldn't walk across the street and today we can almost smell the roses."

"Don't get poetic on me, Jeb Miner." The two were sitting on bench type seats, swaying gently with the movement of the railcar as they made the long haul down from Virginia City to Nevada's capitol, Carson City. The Virginia and Truckee Railroad made travel to Carson City so much easier than in the earlier days. "Though you may be right about the weather."

Corcoran chuckled, remembering just how difficult moving through the streets was. *How many times did I fall, and how many times did I cuss out good old Mother Nature?* "I'll spend some time at the mint, Jeb. You understand what it is I've asked you to do?"

"Of course, Terrence, and I'm more than glad to do it. We'll meet at the station in time to ride the evening express back to town. Did Jackson tell you anything else about this Jaeckes? I think the lack of accent might be more telling than the fact that he was an accomplished faro player."

"I remember listening to my uncle and what Jackson said about a lack of accent, made me think. Uncle Timothy spoke with what Pa said was Chicago blarney. I loved that."

Corcoran had been arguing with himself for several days about whether or not he should pursue this matter that Jaeckes seemed to be behind. Was it really his responsibility? Why wasn't the sheriff doing this? *Well, if the sheriff is involved in the conspiracy, that's why he isn't investigating the conspiracy.* Those kinds of thoughts always made him chuckle. "I'm still wondering why I seem to be the only person in Virginia City that sees collusion. Jeb, the sheriff could fire me if he finds out what I'm doing, and without this little tin badge I wouldn't be able to continue the investigation."

"I think you'd find a way," Miner laughed. "Between Jaeckes and McNabb, we're almost looking at comic opera."

The ride down the mountain wound through the mines and mills in Gold Hill, across a long and high bridge, around American Flats, through some tunnels, and eventually made its way into the Carson River Canyon, skirting the banks of the Carson River. They rode through Empire and the train stopped at the depot in Carson City.

"I'll see you back here, four o'clock sharp, Mr. Miner," Corcoran said. He watched Jeb Miner walk toward the telegraph office. *That accident at the mine really did some damage to that man. He's still just as strong as before, but you can see that every movement hurts. I can't imagine being buried under tons of rock. It must take a very special person to want to work a thousand feet or more underground.* Corcoran would never say it must take a very special kind of person to wear that little tin badge of his.

Corcoran made his way down Carson Street to the U.S. Mint, an impressive building made of locally quarried stone. Great bars of gold and silver from the various mines and mills of the Comstock were sold to the United States government and made their way to the mint where they were turned into coins of the realm, gold and silver. They carried the distinctive CC mintmark and were distributed throughout the west.

There was an equally impressive mint in San Francisco and another in Denver. In the east, there was one in Philadelphia. "They won't let us peons come in and watch the coins being stamped," Corcoran muttered as he walked into the reception area. "Sure, would like to see that."

"May I help you, sir?" The gentleman behind the desk carried a Deputy U.S. Marshal's badge pinned to his vest and could be seen under his suitcoat, and wore an impressive Colt on his hip. There was a double barrel shotgun standing just behind his chair.

"Good morning to you," Corcoran said. "I'm Virginia City Deputy Sheriff Terrence Corcoran, here to see Marshal McBride."

"We've been expecting you, Corcoran. Follow me." They walked deep into the building and up a flight of stairs, down another wide corridor, and into a spacious office. McBride, not too tall but wide and built like a block of the stone used to build the mint, was sitting behind a broad and solid desk.

"Marshal McBride, Deputy Corcoran is here, sir."

"Ah, Corcoran, welcome." He stood and extended a hand across the desk that all but swallowed Corcoran's large hand. "Sit down, sir and tell me all about this little plot you may have uncovered."

Corcoran liked that. Corcoran feared the U.S. Marshal would just laugh at him when he sent the wire asking for a meeting. He didn't lay out the entire problem but offered enough evidence that brought on this get together.

"Thank you, Marshal, it's a pleasure to be here." Corcoran sat down and McBride listened carefully as he spelled out what he thought might be taking place high on the Comstock. It took more than half an hour to spell it all out. "This is most complicated, and when the picture is fully in view, seems less than likely to happen. I just hope I'm not swirling dust with no big rocks under it.

"I'm afraid that I see the district attorney and the sheriff involved in this, that this man called Jaeckes might just be a Chicago crook, and if I'm right, I need lots of help."

"After I got your wire I contacted the Wells Fargo chief of security. Have you left something out of your report, deputy?" McBride had just a wrinkle of a smile on his face when he said this and Corcoran let one form as well.

"I didn't want to give him up," Corcoran said. "A Wells Fargo security agent is in place working as a clerk for the district attorney. His name is Donald Ferguson.

He is also helping Wells Fargo chief clerk Sam Owens feed bad information to Jaeckes."

"I'll say this, Corcoran, you've done your home-work," McBride said. "I think you're right about Jaeckes being a Chicago gangster, but I'm not really sure that the sheriff is involved in the conspiracy. My take on Locatelli is this," the marshal said. McBride leaned forward in his heavy leather covered chair, fastening strong brown eyes on Corcoran.

"He's lazy, not too bright, and won't see the problem even as we're ending the problem." McBride snorted some, stood up, and walked over to a large wood stove and brought the coffee pot and a couple of cups back to his desk.

"Thank you," Corcoran said, taking a mug. "What do you recommend that I do? Jaeckes and McNabb have a number of men working for them, and their plans include at least one wagon and team, and they have something going on north of town near the racetrack."

"You're on the scene, Corcoran. If I send a deputy marshal up there, we might scare them off. You need to keep me informed of anything and everything. You need to work hand in glove with Ferguson. It's impera-tive we keep Mr. Owens alive.

"How secure is the telegraph office? When I got your wire, I was immediately concerned with who else might have seen it. Is there some other way for us to communicate?"

Corcoran sat back in his chair, sipped some coffee and gave the question a little time to ramble around in his head. *He sees the problem. So, I did do the right thing. I like this man.* The big deputy's eyes were shining as he took another sip of coffee and answered the question.

"I believe that Sam Owens sends regular messages for Don Ferguson to Ferguson's chief here. I'm sure he would direct messages to you as well. These are sealed and sent as Wells Fargo material. They wouldn't be as fast as the wires, but they would be secure."

"Good, Corcoran, good. That's how we'll communicate. Keep me fully informed, stay away from McNabb, and don't let Locatelli in on any of this. He isn't smart enough to understand and would certainly blow it up in our faces. It's been a pleasure talking with a real lawman, Corcoran. Keep it up."

Corcoran wanted to chuckle just a bit at that comment. *I guess he doesn't know that I shot the sheriff once. Guess I won't tell him either.* He wouldn't know that Corcoran had been asked to leave Ione, had messed up two saloons Santa Fe, and wasn't welcome in Pioche. *That was just fightin', not law breaking.*

They shook hands and Corcoran made his way back down to the reception desk. He nodded to the deputy and walked out onto Carson City's main street. *Two things, Terrence me boy. Number one, I was right. And number two, it's going to get dangerous. McBride was a step or two ahead of me, I believe and is already working with Wells Fargo security. At least I know somebody will be watching my back, and I hope he's damn good at his job.*

He was chuckling as he made his way across the street and into a saloon that had a sign out front advertising free lunch. He walked up to the bar, got a full mug of cold beer, found a table, and joined a line of men at a buffet table that was filled with meats, cheeses, bread, and other delicacies. "I should venture off that mountain more often," he murmured taking his seat. "I hope Jeb has as much luck as I've had so far today."

He spent the next hour putting away a good meal and digesting an incredible conspiracy unfolding on his watch. *There are two big things that will get in the way of what these hooligans are planning, and the biggest problem for them is what to do with tons of gold and silver coins. If I can figure out what they will attempt to do with all that shiny metal I can bring this problem to a close.*

Corcoran figured it was the men working for Jaeckes that would be the second problem. *Depending on the likes of Tin Cup Duffy and the now One-Armed Lathrop puts a big damper on this project.* He couldn't help not laughing at the thought of those two trying to carry off a heist of this size. "Old swaggering Tin Cup helping One Armed Lathrop move tons of gold and silver while fighting off me and my battalion of tin stars," he murmured, and couldn't help laughing right out loud.

Several people at surrounding tables gave him sidewise glances and he just waved and continued chuckling. "This is a fine mess I'm in," he said to a couple of gents who just continued looking at this strange man with a tin star on his vest.

It was a long ride back to Virginia City and the two men stood on platforms between cars to discuss what each had learned. "You wouldn't believe the size of that marshal. He was just as wide as he was tall and not an ounce of fat on the man. My knuckles still hurt from shaking hands with him."

"Let's go back inside, Terrence. This just hurts too much," Jeb Miner said. They made their way back into the coach and found their seats. "My back and legs have had their month's workout today, old man.

"What did he think of your conspiracy theories?" Jeb Miner was slumped back on the bench and Corcoran could see the pain in his eyes.

"I won't ask you to do this again, Jeb. I didn't realize just how much you still hurt." Miner just waved him off with about half a smile. "Should have brought a flask for a trip like this," Corcoran said. "McBride's a pretty clever fellow, Jeb. I think he's been working with Wells Fargo security for some time and seemed well aware of this plan.

"By the way, Mr. Miner, sir, the plan is not to rob the Bank of California but to take the gold and silver coin shipment coming in for the mines' payrolls. The men get paid every week, but the shipments are only made every six or eight weeks, so we're talking one big poke full of change.

"Just think of it, Mr. Miner. Thousands of men, miners, hoistmen, teamsters, working for all the mines and mills getting paid in gold and silver coins each week. Those shipments must be huge."

Jeb Miner laughed. "What the hell is McNabb going to do with all that metal? Robbing Hank Monk's stage-coach of a hundred-pound strong box is one thing, but stealing a ton or two of gold coins is something else."

"That's been rubbing my head bone all day, Jeb," Corcoran laughed.

Corcoran settled back, watching the Carson River boil through the canyon, filled with the last storm's runoff and thinking about massive crates of gold and silver coinage. He remembered the men in the brewery and that they were building something. He could still see them driving that team north toward Lousetown.

"Why would they go north, Jeb? What was Smithson building in the brewery the other night? Are you close enough to Smithson to get some answers?"

"I doubt the man would even nod my way, Terrence. He knows we're too close. I think you need to take a little ride out to Lousetown, visit the track. No racing this time of year, but there are horses kept at those stables. Skipper Johnson's brother Washington takes care of the stables."

"Sounds like a plan to me. I wish I could trust Locatelli, but McBride insisted that I keep him in the dark. I need somebody to ride with me," Corcoran said. "First choice would be Don Ferguson, but that too would be no. Damn me."

"You're missing the obvious, Terrence. Take Skipper with you. Nobody messes with the Johnson brothers."

That brought another round of laughter from the two men. "Talk about a lot of weight," Corcoran said. Skipper Johnson and his brother Washington, sons of a former slave couple that was set free during the big war, were enormous, tall, wide, and as strong as mules. "Those boys test the mettle of any horse they mount."

"WHERE HAVE YOU BEEN, CORCORAN?" Sheriff Emilio Locatelli was in a rage when Corcoran waltzed into the office. "You're supposed to relieve me at four, not six. I've had to put one of the Gold Hill deputies on your shift. Answer me." His eyes were fierce and Corcoran was sure another kick to his tender place might be in the offing.

"I had a personal problem, sheriff, and no way to get hold of you. It won't happen again." Corcoran hoped that would suffice but didn't really believe it would. *This is awkward. I don't much care for lying to my boss but I surely can't tell him what I was doing. Hell, he'd shoot me.* That almost brought a chuckle up, and he quashed it quickly.

"Why don't you sleep in tomorrow, sheriff? I'll stay a couple of hours over." He poured some coffee and watched Locatelli get into his heavy coat. "I mean it," he said again. "It won't happen again." Locatelli gave a grumpy goodbye slamming the door on his way out.

Corcoran was exhausted as he sat behind the big desk. "I haven't had a minute's sleep since sometime yesterday morning, but I'm sure glad I made that trip to Carson. I think I'll pop in on Suzanna and have supper then find Skipper Johnson. Jeb was right, get those Johnson boys on my side and we'll all be safe."

"EVENING, SUZANNA," he said, finding his way to a table near the east windows of the café. "I need one of your platters full of steaks and potatoes. And a gallon of coffee." Her smile back could have lit the stage at Piper's Opera House.

"You're very tired, Terrence. Is everything all right with you?" *What kind of a man is this Terrence Corcoran? He seems so light hearted most of the time, yet carries the weight of the world on his shoulders. Be careful, little lady,* she admonished herself, but couldn't help the feelings that were building in her.

"Just been a bit busy," he said. "I had a little personal business to take care of in Carson City, so I didn't get any sleep today. I'll make up for it tomorrow morning, though." He watched her go into the kitchen wishing he could find some way to spend some time with her, alone.

The conspiracy came back in a flash when Tin Cup Duffy slithered up to his table. "Duffy. I haven't seen your mug around for a day or two. You still hanging around with the duke of purple velvet?"

"He's European royalty and you shouldn't talk about him that way. He pays me well for my efforts, Terrence. You were wrong being rude to the man. You'll see."

Corcoran was sure that Tin Cup was about to say something else, and seemed to catch himself. *Was he going to tell me about the duke's plans to rob the coin shipment? Or about what was going on out at Lousetown?*

"Have you seen Clarence Boyington in the last few days, Tin Cup? I need to have a talk with him."

"I saw him just the other night, Terrence, and he feels very bad about pulling that gun on you. He would really like to apologize, if you'd let him."

"I bet he does," Corcoran chuckled. "You tell that fool I'll be making my rounds as soon as I've had supper. Now go away. I want to eat alone and in silence." Suzanna brought his supper and never said a word to Duffy as he walked from the café.

"He's not a very nice man, Terrence. You'd do well to stay away from him. He and Orin Lathrop are involved in something ugly with Mr. Jaeckes, and I don't want you to be like them."

It was a wonderful feeling that surged through Corcoran when she said that and he reached out and took her hand, holding it with both of his. "The only way I would be with them is when I arrest them and shove them into a cold jail cell, Suzanna. Has Lathrop said something to you? Something that frightens you? I wouldn't want that."

"Just seeing either one of them frightens me, Terrence. You enjoy your supper. I've work to do, others to take care of." *But I'd much rather just stand here holding your hand.*

CORCORAN FOUGHT it for a half hour or so after his large supper and finally said "deep enough," a term used by miners when they are quitting their jobs. He slipped up to Miner's and found his bed, and just flopped across it. *Just a couple of hours and I'll be fine.* It was close to midnight when Jeb Miner shook him awake.

'So, this is how you protect our fine city, is it," he jibed. "The town's quiet, but I thought you would rather be out there in the cold and danger, than all cuddled up in a feather bed with warm blankets."

"You're a cruel man, Jeb Miner," Corcoran said. He slowly came awake, found he even still had his boots on, and stood, stretching for the ceiling. "I do feel better, though. Anyone besides you miss me out there?"

"Old man Flanders from Gold Hill made a round or two and went back down to slippery gulch. How long has that man been a deputy?"

"Nigh on to a hunnert years, I think," Corcoran said. "Well, I'll see you in the morning, Jeb. My first job tonight is finding Skipper Johnson. That was a fine idea of yours, sir. Sleep well."

Corcoran walked the length of C Street, from the Divide to Mill Street, and then down to D Street to find Mr. Johnson. Very few people were out on a cold night, but at least it wasn't snowing and the wind wasn't howling. "There you are, Skipper. I've been looking for you. How about we find a cup of coffee somewhere?"

"It will have to be my shack or yours, Corcoran. They won't let me in most of those places uptown." There were definite color and social lines in Virginia City, and Negroes like Skipper Washington were banned from many of the businesses. Many of the Chinese were banned as well. It was many years after the end of the war, and while the black man might be free in the eyes of the law, he wasn't necessarily welcomed in Virginia City.

They settled in Skipper Johnson's one room shack, tucked behind one of the working girl's cribs. The wood stove was hot, the coffee strong enough to scrape a hog with, and Corcoran spent an hour talking with Johnson.

"You know, they would kill me before they'd kill you, Terrence. You're asking an awful lot." He sat back in his chair and reached over to the table to pour some whiskey into his coffee cup. Corcoran took some too. "I'll ride out to Lousetown with you, but not tomorrow. I got to clean Miss Cindy's rooms tomorrow.

"I don't know what Washington will say, but you've always been fair with me, I don't like McNabb or Tin Cup at all, and that Mr. Jaeckes has said some vile things to me more than once." He sat back and laughed long, giving Corcoran a slap on the knee.

"You know he's not any kind of royalty, European or otherwise. He's right straight out of the slaughterhouses of Chicago, Terrence. He's a phony from the first word. Yeah, I'll work with you. You promise you'll continue working to find Miss Donnegan's killer?"

"I am working on that, Skipper. When I get off shift day after tomorrow, we'll ride out to Lousetown. Try your best to get Washington to throw in with us. Even though I'm wearing a badge, I'm doing this without the sheriff knowing about it, so we won't have any legal protection."

CHAPTER 11

"IT'S COLD OUT THERE, MICHAEL," CORCORAN SAID, shucking his buffalo robe coat. "Would you have a hot brandy, by chance?" He knew Orin Lathrop would not try to look him up, he knew that Clarence Boyington was in hiding with him, and he knew he needed more help than the Johnson brothers could give. *Donald Ferguson can't do anything without jeopardizing his undercover work, Sam Owens simply can't do anything but gather information, and I need a couple of guns walking alongside this old son of Erin. Maybe I'll just shuck the whole idea of upholding the law and run away with the dear lady, Suzanna O'Meara.*

"All right, Terrence, come out of your dream world and talk to me." Donahue asked him twice if he was going to stand at the bar or take a seat and got no response. Finally, he rapped his knuckles on the bar and Corcoran stood straight up.

"Sorry, Mr. Donahue. Things are getting to me and I don't have any help. What's the word on the street now that people can get around some? Anyone talking about Lousetown? Or our friend the duke?"

"Too early in the year to be talking about racing, Terrence." Donahue was obviously not aware of what might be happening north of town. "No, haven't heard a word about Lousetown. There's always talk about the duke. What about you? You look like the wrath, by the way."

"Thank you for that," Corcoran chuckled. "No sleep yesterday." He took a long drink of hot brandy and settled back in his chair. "How long has Ike Smithson been tight with the criminal element? He wasn't when I left town two years ago. But he's been doing some kind of work with Lathrop, Boyington, and Duffy, and got a little snarly with me the other night. He isn't the same Ike Smithson I remember."

"He lost his wife while you were gone and blames Locatelli. Dan Small, you remember that idiot I'm sure, tried to stick up old Fred Hastings at the gun shop and it got rather wild. "

"I remember Small alright. Every time I turned around the fool was pulling a gun on somebody. He should have been sent to prison years ago," Corcoran said.

"Locatelli stormed in, guns drawn, Small took two shots at him before the sheriff gunned him down. One of Small's shots killed Elsa Smithson as she walked down C Street on the other side of the street.

"Smithson hasn't been the same since. People swear that Locatelli came in with his gun drawn but didn't fire until Small took two shots at him. There's some serious bad blood between Smithson and the sheriff. You tying him into this plot of Jaeckes'?"

"It's all a jumbled-up mess, Michael. I won't let man get that first shot," Corcoran said, then almost turned a slight deeper color in the cheeks remembering that Boyington not only pulled a gun on him, but got in a shot. He looked a bit sheepish on the one hand and angry as a bee denied a fresh spring blossom as he stood up and grabbed his old coat.

"I better wander about some, justify my large wage. Keep your ears open for me." He put his heavy coat on and headed into the cold. *Locatelli has such a small force, and even if he had more deputies I don't know if I could trust them. Just four of us in town and two in Gold Hill. One extra gun on my side would be good, two would be better.*

Often when Corcoran had thoughts like this buzzing around in his head he wondered why it was he even carried a badge. He told people in Austin that he was coming back to Virginia City to work in one of the mines, that he was tired of trying to catch the bad guys. In Ione he was run out of town taking one of the bad guys down.

Don't ever remember anyone walking up to me and saying thankee for lettin' them ugly outlaws shoot at my or for me whuppin' on 'em and flinging 'em into the pokey hole. My next job is gonna be chasing some dumb old cows around some pretty mountains. There will be tall grass, no snow, no wind, and no bad guys. And I'll be bored out of my ever-lovin mind.

"I THINK we have our plans all in order, McNabb. Those

boys in Lousetown have done a fine job." Ezra McNabb was settled in a comfortable leather chair in Elon Jaeckes' suite in the International Hotel getting an update from his partner. "We'll be able to hide those wagons with ease."

"I hope you're right. It's the only thing that would foul up this plan of ours. Have you actually seen what's been done or are you taking that fool Tin Cup at his word?" McNabb feared that Jaeckes was easily swayed by fast talkers and Duffy certainly fit that description.

"Both Duffy and Lathrop assure me that three wagons will fit in the tunnels and the portal can't be seen, even if one is close." Jaeckes never liked being questioned about how he handled his responsibilities and stiffened some at McNabb's comment. "I was planning to take a carriage ride through the area tomorrow or the next day to see for myself."

"That's a good idea, Elon," McNabb said. "There are three men coming in this week from Denver, supposedly to look for business property for sale. Remember, we talked about them several weeks ago. They will be staying here at the International. They will be the primary gunmen, but it will be best if we're not seen associating with them, publicly."

"Good. They were highly recommended." He looked around the room, just to make sure they were alone. "I'm still not sure that three gunmen, as good as these three are reputed to be, is going to be enough. Duffy, Smithson, and Boyington are all good with guns, meaning they can hit a target, but they aren't gunmen that kill people. They will also be driving the wagons. Since Lathrop got his arm shot off, we'll have to use him as a distraction. All we need now is word from that Wells Fargo clerk on when the shipment will be coming."

"Those three guns coming to town are more than a match for what little protection that will be in place. Everyone else will be good for distraction and if they do hit someone, all the better." McNabb chortled.

"It's important that we get Locatelli involved somehow. The general public must be made to believe that he was behind the robbery. He needs to be near the depot when those wagons are loaded, and then shot before he can react. We have to make it look like one of the guards shot him." McNabb had an ugly grin on his face and took a long swig of brandy.

"We'll have someone near the depot wearing a badge, being seen, and responding to the heist by shooting the sheriff. That will implicate him and get me off the menu. I won't be near that depot and neither should you, Elon."

"What about that deputy, Corcoran? I tried to enlist his help," Jaeckes said, "and he turned me down flat. I'll shoot him myself, but will he get in the way? He's been asking a lot of questions."

"He's just a dumb Irisher, Elon. I'll have the sheriff send him on a mission somewhere on delivery day. Not to worry."

"How much money was McNabb talking about?" Lefty Smith was standing at the long bar at the Browns Hotel in Denver, sipping some fine bourbon. Smith arrived in Denver the day before and was fighting the effects of a severe hangover. He came on the train from Chicago, was a heavy drinker, and arriving in Denver hit the bar immediately. Drinking heavy at a mile above sea level after coming from the Great Lakes all but put him under the table. There just isn't enough oxygen in the atmosphere to burn off all that alcohol.

"Keep your thoughts on the money, Lefty, and your head won't hurt so much," Hal Dolan laughed. "You know McNabb and Jaeckes and their big talk about money. The wire I got said we'd be set for years." Dolan spent most of his time dodging bounty hunters after killing two Texas Rangers several months ago. He came north hoping the pressure would be off.

"He may have something this time, Dolan." The third man, Poncho Suarez, up from El Paso, was known for carrying twin revolvers and a sawed off double barrel shotgun. "He's going to take a gold shipment coming from the Carson City mint and all he needs us for is gunning down the guards."

"Just gunning down the guards?" Dolan laughed, but it was a derisive laugh, not mirthful. "Do you know who guards those shipments? It's U.S. Marshals, not dumbass deputy sheriffs. He really does need us," and this time the laugh was filled with mirth.

"Let's make sure he pays us well," Lefty Smith said. "What time does our train leave?"

"We're scheduled out of here at one o'clock, so drink up and let's get going." Dolan wasn't named the leader he simply took command and the other two let him. They put their luggage in a cab and were driven to the station. "McNabb sent our tickets and it appears we have good sleeper berths. Maybe the guy knows what he's doing this time."

"I hope they have a good club car," is all Lefty Smith said.

"The swaying back and forth of the car should be good for your stomach," Poncho Suarez laughed. Smith dropped his hand near the butt of his big revolver and Dolan quickly stepped in front of him.

"No, Lefty." He turned to Suarez. "No more of that. We might not like each other, but if we work together we might just end up very rich." Lefty eased his big left hand back away from the weapon, but Poncho walked off with a sly grin on his face. It would be a long several days to Virginia City.

CHAPTER 12

"Were you able to get word to Washington that we'd be visiting?" Corcoran and Skipper Johnson were riding down D Street and would follow the road through the north end of Seven Mile Canyon, over a ridge and drop into a long valley. It was an easy ride most of the time, but the remnants of that last blizzard were still evident in drifts, ice, and uprooted Piñon pine. It wasn't warm enough to be muddy.

"He knows I'm comin'," Johnson grinned. "You'll be a bit of a surprise." Johnson was laughing loud, picturing the look that might be on his brother's face when he rides up with a white deputy sheriff.

Corcoran's first thought was that he wasn't big on surprises and he hoped that Washington Johnson was. "I've never had to arrest him or give him a hassle, so let's hope for the best. I want you to know exactly what it is I'm looking at," Corcoran said. "There's going to be a big problem soon, and I need back up." He told Skipper Johnson part of the problem two nights before, but took the time to fully expand on the subject during the ride north.

Mornings in northern Nevada are usually cold, but gorgeous. They were riding across the eastern flank of Sun Mountain, looking out across the Carson Plain, could follow the course of the Carson River all the way to its sink. The sun was blasting its torrent of heat their way, but Corcoran was sure it petered out well before it reached the two men.

"Looks like we're gonna get a few days of nice weather, Skipper. Your brother has a nice little ranch out here, takes care of the racecourse stables, eh? Ever thought of running a ranch?"

"Did some dirt farmin' down in Texas before coming to Nevada. Don't know if it was the people around me or the dirt itself that I didn't much care for. Old Washington, though, he surely did like the dirt."

"I get your point," Corcoran laughed. "I'm gonna give up the badge and spend my time with cows, I think." *Suzanna O'Meara would be the best to spend lots of time with rather than cows. Skipper doesn't need to know that.*

The mountain range that Virginia City is perched on runs north and south as do most in Nevada, and is an ancient range. The valleys and mountain sides are filled with rocks, most of the dirt having washed away thousands if not millions of years ago. Even the alluvial flows are washed-clean rocks. What growth exists is scrub piñon, scrub cedar, sage, and rabbit brush. Because of that Washington Johnson saw the two riders a full half hour before they arrived at his shack.

"Didn't say you was bringin' John Law," Washington rasped. He was two years older than Skipper and larger by some. Skipper was a big man, Washington was huge in every way; tall, heavy, strong. He filled the doorway of his shack, a shotgun carried with ease and a side arm stuck in his belt. Corcoran's closer look showed a Bowie knife sticking out of his right boot.

"Corcoran's a good man, Washington. You know that, and he's been good to me always. We need to talk, brother."

"Coffee's on, flask is filled, and my ears still work. Step down and welcome, Terrence Corcoran. You've always treated me right, but you are the man, the law, and I haven't always gotten along with your kind. If my brother wants me to listen, I will. Come in," he said, that voice as raspy as a blue-jay's and as loud as a mule's bray.

Corcoran found the Johnson cabin to be just one large room with a cast iron cook stove at one end, a table and four chairs near it, and a homemade rope bed at the other end with a wooden box holding a lamp. There were doors opposite each other and windows on the other two walls.

Corcoran had to hold himself to keep from asking about the rope used for the bed. *If that rope will hold that man in comfort, it must be what they use to tie up the big ships in Boston.*

The cabin was small but more than tidy, it was very clean, with curtains at the windows, and a quilt spread over the bed. There were paintings in home-made frames on the walls. The lamps were not the barn style, rather more delicate and attractive. "You have a nice home, Washington," Corcoran said. "Those paintings and frames. Did you do those?"

Washington Johnson strode over to one, had a grand smile on his face, and touched the frame with a huge finger. "Our mama painted this one," he said. "The other two were done by our sister when we lived down near New Orleans. I can't paint worth nothin'," he smiled. "But I did make the frames."

"You do beautiful work," Corcoran said.

It was two hours later the three men stepped out of the shack into bright sunshine, its warmth melting the lingering snow fast. "Looks like more company," Washington said, pointing south. They saw two mounted riders and a well-appointed buggy being drawn by a team coming along the main road.

That road led to the racetrack just a mile further north. Washington's little pathway off the main road extended east into the rocky bottom of a hillside, and further along the main road north was another little trail that also led off into that hillside. "Let's move those horses around behind the shack and not be seen," Washington Johnson said. "After what you said inside, Corcoran, I'm gonna start bein' a little more careful."

They moved their mounts to a small corral behind the cabin and walked into a grove of scrub pine to watch the party moving north. "That's Jaeckes in the buggy, driven by that monster guard of his," Corcoran said. "He's bigger than both you Johnson boys together. That looks like Tin Cup and Ike Smithson riding alongside.

"Here's what I want to do," Corcoran said. "I'm going to follow them, and you fellers stay here. When I find out what they're up to I'll come back and tell you. This way, in case I'm seen, you won't appear to be involved." The Johnson brothers nodded agreement right away, and Corcoran slipped back around the cabin and mounted his horse. After Jaeckes' group rode by, Corcoran came out onto the main road, following about a half mile behind.

"Even if I can't see them, that buggy and team is leaving some good track to follow," he chuckled. Jaeckes and company didn't seem to worry about being followed or being seen. They continued north and turned east before reaching the racetrack. Corcoran held up and let them move considerably ahead of him.

I wonder just what's up that little trail they're on? He hadn't ridden on that path before but could see that it meandered its way through the sage and scrub brush, then up into the ridge, a couple of miles distant. The riders weren't in any apparent hurry and Corcoran took the time to try and understand what was happening.

If Jaeckes is just a Chicago gangster as so many seem to believe, and if McNabb and Locatelli are in cahoots with him, what is it that would bring them out here? The plan is to steal the mint shipment when it arrives in Virginia City and then what? They have to do more that kill the guards and take the shipment. What are they going to do with those wagons full of gold and silver coins? "It ain't like they just throw a saddlebag of goodies on the back of horse," he blurted right out, caught himself, and laughed at what he was thinking.

He almost snickered picturing them driving the wagons up to C Street and turning down the main street and riding out of town. Or making a dash down

Six Mile Canyon? That would take them to the main emigrant road from the east to California. Jumbo grade would take them to Washoe City. No matter how they tried to leave the Comstock they would be riding into well populated areas, and with the wagons, would stand out like a red flag in a field of bulls.

As the little group neared the first ridgeline of the hills rearing up from the valley floor, Corcoran could see indications of some earthwork. "A mine? Out here? What on earth are these people up to?" They were about half a mile ahead of him and he pulled his horse off the trail and rode to a small stand of piñons, tied off, and watched for a minute or two.

Corcoran pulled his rifle from the scabbard and started walking toward what appeared to be a pair of tunnels into the mountainside. He kept low and tried to keep bushes and trees between himself and the site. No one in the group seemed to be watching for visitors and this allowed Corcoran to get fairly close quickly.

He spotted the large wagon that ran off from behind the brewery the other night, saw what looked like large timbers stacked nearby, and noticed that the tunnel entrances were much larger than normal.

Those mine entrances are really oversized. You could drive a team of four pulling large wagons right inside. Oh, my, he almost said out loud. He scrambled back to his horse and quickly rode back to the Johnson cabin. *"I've got to get back to town. I would not believe what I just saw.*

He stopped long enough to tell the Johnson brothers what he saw, explained what he thought Jaeckes's plan might be, and hightailed it to Virginia City.

CORCORAN STEPPED off his horse and tied him to the hitch rail in front of the Wells Fargo building, and jumped up on the boardwalk. He waited for a couple of people to walk by and entered the large building at C and Taylor. "Sam Owens in? I need to see him right away," he said to the clerk behind the long desk. He wiped sweat from his face despite the cold temperatures.

"In his office, Terrence. Looks like you've been riding hard."

"Thanks," Corcoran said and pushed his way through a swinging gate and walked down a hallway that led to Owens' office. It was sparse, a simple desk with a couple of chairs in front and Owens sitting behind. There was a file cabinet, some maps on the walls, and one window opening to the backside of a building.

"Sam, remember what I said how Marshal McBride wants us to get messages to him? We need to get one to him soonest." Corcoran didn't wait for an answer and sat down across from Owens. He used a piece of paper on the desk and started writing. It took just a few minutes for him to write out what he wanted McBride to know.

"This needs to go on your next package to Carson City."

"No problem, Terrence." Owens picked up the message and read it before putting it in an envelope. "Are you sure about this?"

"I was just there, Sam. Have you heard anything about this?"

"Ike Smithson has had several men working night

shifts for weeks now. Everyone has assumed he was building a new brewery or maybe even a distillery. The men working for him never say what they're doing."

"We know now," Corcoran chuckled. "Make sure that note gets to McBride just as soon as possible. Any news on when that shipment is coming? What is it, six to eight weeks between shipments?"

"Because of security, they never tell me until it's on its way. I usually have about twelve hours to arrange for wagons and teams. All the security details are taken care of by the folks in Carson. I get the wagons and teams, notify the sheriff and the bank, and that's it."

"Make sure I'm on that list, Sam. Is Locatelli always notified? Does he provide deputies at the site or along the route from the depot to the bank?"

"Sheriff Locatelli informed us just before the last shipment that he wanted to be on the notification list." Sam Owens had a worried look on his face as he continued. "Wells Fargo has several men, the marshals are always on hand, and the bank has several men on hand. It's just recent that the sheriff and one deputy are also on hand, but do more watching than anything. Like it's a holiday."

"Might be real fireworks this time," Corcoran said. He walked out, mounted his horse and rode back to the courthouse to start his regular shift. *I gotta learn to set aside just a few hours each day to sleep. This is getting out of hand.* He walked into the courthouse and noticed that Donald Ferguson was still at his desk.

Corcoran caught his attention and indicated that they needed to talk and got a nod back from the D.A.'s assistant. Corcoran went across the hall and into the sheriff's office, slipping out of his heavy coat. "Evening sheriff," he said. "Looks like you kept the town in one piece, again." He grabbed the coffee pot and a cup.

"Is there any truth to the rumor running through town that Jaeckes may not be a European duke, that he might be from Chicago?" The sheriff asked and caught Corcoran just starting to pour his coffee. "Heard that twice today."

Corcoran wondered where this might be going. *If Locatelli is connected to McNabb, then he knows that Jaeckes is from Chicago. Unless McNabb has held that back. McNabb is a slippery little devil and might be setting Locatelli up to take the heat when the big heist takes place.*

"There's been a lot of talk about our velvet wearing duke, sheriff. I've met the man and he's as phony as a wooden nickel. He's in Virginia City for a reason and I would bet a lot of my high wage that whatever the reason is, it's against the law."

Locatelli said the city was his, put on his coat and headed out the door. Corcoran threw more wood in the stove and poured another cup of coffee. He sat behind the desk, found Locatelli's flask and poured some good whiskey in the cup. *We've added another layer on the Jaeckes' mystery. If Locatelli is tied in with McNabb he would certainly know all about our fine faux royal. I need a long talk with Mr. Ferguson, and somewhere that we would not be seen.*

Ten minutes later Ferguson stepped into the office. "McNabb just left and I saw the sheriff leave. Can we talk?"

"It's not safe anywhere around this old building, Donald. Have you ever been out to the Chinese cemetery late at night? I've a hankering to be there, say about three o'clock in the morning. And it's imperative that you have these same feelings, deep in your ever-loving soul."

"I do, Terrence. I do," Ferguson said. "Well, have a good night," he said, maybe a little too loud, and walked out of the courthouse. Corcoran smiled quietly, finished his coffee, grabbed his coat and headed out the door.

CORCORAN MADE the rounds of town, spoke to half a dozen people and worked his way to the Silver Dollar Café and a much-needed full meal. "Suzanna darlin', I haven't eaten in days, at least I can't remember eating."

"You need to take better care of yourself, Terrence Corcoran. You men seem to think you're indestructible and you're not. I'm bringing you a big roast of pork shoulder and a pot or two of potato soup, and you better eat all of it." Her eyes were blazing but Corcoran could see the little grin that was trying to hide behind the strong words.

"You need a good woman, Corcoran," she whispered to herself.

"I won't leave a smidgin' on the platter, dear girl." The café was more than half filled, mostly day shift miners in for their evening meal. He noticed there were a few families, something that was being seen more and more in the old mining camp. Many of the men were dressed as for Sunday meeting and the women were in their finest. *Our town is growing up, I'm afraid. A strong economy does that to a place.*

"I understand there's a wonderful performance

scheduled at John Piper's this Sunday, Suzanna. Would you be kind enough to join me? Maybe we could enjoy a good meal at the International Hotel after."

"Why, Mr. Corcoran, I would indeed be honored to be seen with you," she was blushing, and truth be told, so was Terrence Corcoran.

"I'll pick you up at two, then. This was a fine meal. I'll still be on shift when you close. May I escort you home?"

"Yes, Terrence, you may. I'll close at eleven."

Corcoran's feet never really touched the boardwalk as he made his way south to the Washoe Club and an after-supper brandy with Jeb Miner. "Ah, Terrence. There's a gentleman at the bar you may wish to engage in conversation. He's the one in the dovetail coat and top hat."

"He looks more like a drummer than a gentleman. What's his game, Jeb?"

"He has some jewelry to sell, and with what is being said up and down these streets of silver, you may want to see some of it."

"And just what would you be implying sir?"

Miner laughed and simply said, "Suzanna."

Corcoran huffed a bit but couldn't hold back a smile either, and walked up to the bar, standing next to the man in the dovetail coat. "A brandy, Tommy, to ease my supper into place." He looked at the man standing next to him and saw a thin, gaunt man with sallow skin stretched taught across his cheeks and chin. He wore no facial hair, and his mouth seemed turned down permanent. If he was armed it was well hidden.

"Good evening. I don't believe we've met. I'm Corcoran, Deputy Terrence Corcoran."

"Good evening to you, Deputy Corcoran. My name's John Moran, recently of Denver. This is my first visit to the home of the fabled Comstock Lode. Much of the jewelry I offer may have once found a home under these streets."

"Jewelry, eh? Are you planning to open a business in our fair community?"

"No, I sell privately. If you would be interested in some fine gold and silver, diamonds and emeralds, I'm lodged at the International Hotel, third floor. I'm showing another gentleman in half an hour, buying from another at about eleven, and will be available to show after midnight."

"I may just knock on your door, sir." Corcoran drank his brandy and stepped back over to Jeb Miner's table with a second.

"Have you had any sleep in the last few days, Terrence?"

"Not that I'm aware of," he said. He plopped down in the chair and wondered just how much of what he had learned he should relate to Miner. "There's trouble, not on the horizon, but right here where we're sitting, Jeb." He took a bare sip of the drink, thinking that if he had more than these two he would lay his head on the table and sleep till dawn.

"I think I know what McNabb and Locatelli are up to. I'm now positive of their plans to rob the Wells Fargo shipment when it arrives, but the one thing that's been bothering me is what would they do with it when they get it?"

"That's been on my mind too, Terrence. It has to be gotten out of town, and there's no place to go." He was almost chuckling when he said that. "What a fiasco that would be. Hundred thousand dollars in gold and silver and no way to get it out of town."

"I think I know their plan and I sent a note to the marshals in Carson City. I'll hear back from them and let you know what's going on. Hear anything more on our friend the velvet duke?"

"I got answers back after our trip to Carson City. He's a wanted criminal out of Chicago. The wires I sent to Chicago were answered within a day, Terrence. He's strictly a con man. No murders or attempted murders in his background, but numerous arrests for robbery, armed robbery, loan sharking.

"I included McNabb in my wires, and he's a known associate but does not have a record of arrests or convictions. He's an attorney tied very tight to Chicago's criminal interests. They are a team, Terrence."

"I doubt if Locatelli knows any of this," Corcoran murmured, wondering just how deep the sheriff was in this conspiracy. "I wish I trusted the man enough to bring all of this to his attention. I really believe that he's up to his neck with McNabb. At least we have the marshals on our side. I better get out there and protect this fine law-abiding community of ours." He wondered why he didn't pass along the information about the twin mines or about the Johnson brothers? *Jeb Miner is a good friend, and he's helping at every opportunity, but right now I don't trust anyone but myself.*

"Even if they can hide that shipment in those tunnels," he muttered, making his way back to the courthouse, "it will take months for them to move it about into safe places. This is an incredibly stupid operation. Each man involved will be paid off in those coins and the rest will have to be moved by Jaeckes, McNabb, and Locatelli. How?"

"You look as tired as I feel, Terrence," Suzanna said. They were slowly walking up Union Street to B Street. They would turn south for two long blocks. "It was a busy night. It seems like everyone in town wanted to eat out." They walked in silence for a few minutes, enjoying the cold winter air, seeing billions of stars winking at them. She could feel that Corcoran had a lot more on his mind than walking a lovely lass home.

"There are problems, dear girl, and I'm not sure when I'll get a full sleep. Do you know Daniel McKenzie? He's the boss at the Miners' Union, and may have taken a fancy to much of the union's money." She nodded that she knew who he was. "If you should happen to see him in the next few days, get word to me, if you would."

"I heard rumors about that," she said. "He's a pleasant man, but always very quiet. Always sits alone by the windows. Like you do," she laughed. They were holding hands, walking along the deserted B Street, enjoying this time together.

He didn't want to talk about what he was most worried about and instead talked about his family and the times he had growing up. She enjoyed that and spent time doing the same, and it took a little longer than would be normal to make the walk. "I think we should do this a bit more often, Miss O'Meara. Probably every night."

Suzanna chuckled and squeezed his hand. "It is most pleasant, sir. Please try to get some rest." He wanted to wrap his arms around the lady, wanted to swarm her with warmth and love, but instead simply watched her open the door to her home and walk in. He made sure she was in and safe, and walked back north along B Street to the International Hotel.

CHAPTER 13

"John Moran," Corcoran said softly, as he made his way north along B Street. The International Hotel snuggled right up to the mountainside with an entrance on C Street and then another entrance up the hill on B Street. The C Street level housed more than one gentleman's bar, some gaming rooms, and restaurants. The B Street level was used more often by the ladies of the community.

"I wonder where this Moran feller gets this jewelry he sells privately?" Corcoran was holding a full conversation with himself as he walked. "I'll not buy anything but I'll be most interested in seeing just what this man has to offer. I wouldn't know fake gold from the real stuff I'm afraid." He was chuckling to himself as he entered the hotel from B Street.

He took the stairs to the third floor rather than the newfangled elevator everyone talked about and found Moran's room. "Good evening again, Mr. Moran."

"Corcoran," he said, not showing the slightest smile. "Come in, please. Will you join me in a brandy?"

"No thank you, I've still got several hours to go tonight. Tell me about this jewelry business of yours. I'd think having an actual store would be more conducive to jewelry sales."

"I'm afraid you'd be wrong, sir." He walked over to a heavy and ornate table that had been brought to his rooms. It was covered in a splendid cloth that seemed to have gold and silver threads woven in, and some of the colors reminded one of emeralds, rubies, pearls, and diamonds. Moran opened a case that was filled with gold, silver, and jewels. "I come to busy and successful towns and cities like this one and let the leading citizens know I'm not just selling, I'm buying as well." Corcoran wondered if that might stimulate a few members of the criminal society to make a midnight requisition or two?

Virginia City is not just a successful little town it is a wealthy city with many citizens having extreme wealth, often displaying that wealth. That's what keeps men like Lathrop and Tin Cup in business. He decided that he would want to see everything that might be in that case.

"My stock is changing constantly and I have only the finest of items for sale. I'm very discriminating in what I buy, too." He spread items across the table. There were necklaces, bracelets, brooches, rings, and everything any lady or gentleman could want. "This will give you an idea."

Corcoran was amazed at what he was looking at when a second thought flashed across his quick mind. *There is no security here. Anyone could walk through that door, shoot this fool, and walk out with thousands of dollars in gold and jewels.* "Where is your security, Mr. Moran?

Why don't you have an armed guard with you and your wares?"

"I've never found it necessary, deputy. No one would rob me in a hotel this fine." Corcoran scoffed at that and decided this Moran was just a simple fool. He walked closer to the table to get a better look at the merchandise.

Corcoran picked up a necklace, looking at it carefully. He tried to keep a neutral look on his face as he examined the gold and emerald piece. "That is one of my finer pieces," Moran said. Corcoran laid it back down on the table and carefully turned to the drummer.

"Where did you get this piece, sir?"

"Oh, I'm not sure," he stammered. "Maybe Denver, maybe St. Louis. It is beautiful."

"It is indeed," Corcoran said. He pulled his big forty-five revolver and cocked the hammer back. "Turn around, sir, and put your hands behind your back."

"What is this? A deputy is robbing me?" He started to make a move and Corcoran slapped him across the side of the head with the heavy weapon. The man fell to the carpet immediately and Corcoran rolled him onto his stomach and put handcuffs on him. He jerked him to his feet and pushed him onto the bed. *Hotel won't appreciate the blood on the bedspread, and I'm sure the county will get the bill*, but he wasn't chuckling a bit.

"You're under arrest for the murder of Claire Donnegan." He stepped to the table and lifted the necklace again, seeing the beautiful shamrock with the emerald in the middle hanging from a gold chain. Moran was starting to come around and Corcoran allowed the man to regain conscience before asking him anything. He took those few minutes to look at some of the other jewelry.

"Seems obvious that most of this is used," he murmured. "I wonder how many dead bodies might be connected to some of this beauty." The only word that kept flowing through his mind was how elegant it all was, and yet how vile it was really. He had the revolver holstered and got the man on his feet.

"Where's the room key?" Moran nodded toward the dresser near the door and Corcoran pushed the man in that direction, found the key, and when they were in the hallway, Corcoran locked the door, putting the key in his pocket. "Let's go," he said, pushing the man forward.

Many eyes watched Corcoran escort Moran, hand-cuffed and bleeding through the hotel and out onto the street for the short march to the courthouse. He pushed the man into a chair near the desk, got more wood stuffed into the stove and poured a cup of coffee. "So, Mr. Moran, I believe the question was, where did you get that particular necklace?" He picked up a short baton and smacked his open hand with it a couple of times. "Unless you want another knot on your stupid head, you'd best answer the question."

"I bought it yesterday," Moran whimpered. "What did you mean when you said murder?"

Corcoran ignored the question. "Who did you buy that necklace from?" He continued to whack his open hand with the hardwood baton.

"I don't know the man's name. He only had one arm, I remember. I didn't kill anyone. If that necklace was stolen, I didn't steal it." He was talking fast, trying his best to make a quick sale, Corcoran thought.

He's probably telling the truth right about now but I'm going to press him some more. It sounds like good old Orin Lathrop is back in the news. "Tell me about this one-armed man who sold you the necklace. How much did you pay for it?"

"My hands are going to sleep. Can you take the cuffs off? I won't try to run. I didn't kill anyone or even hurt anyone. I bought the necklace for a double eagle from the man. He said it was his mother's and he needed the money. Please?"

A double eagle? Twenty dollars? I'da snapped it up myself at that price. Poor Claire, my beautiful present stolen, you dead, and Lathrop gets twenty bucks. He'll also get a short rope off a high porch.

Corcoran walked around the desk and took the handcuffs off the man, poured him a cup of coffee and sat back down. "I don't know why I believe you, but I think I do. I'm going to book you into our little jail, Mr. Moran, more for your protection than anything else, and take all your jewelry and other possessions into custody as evidence.

"You're in possession of stolen property, sir. That necklace was owned by one of our doves who was killed recently in a savage attack. The man you described as selling it to you is a known criminal in the area and I'll track him down and bring him in, too. After that, hopefully the court will see to it that Mr. Lathrop hangs from a high cottonwood tree, and we'll let the court decide what to do with you. If you're the least bit involved in Claire Donnegan's death, you will hang.

"Drink your coffee, and I'm gonna lock you up, sir."

IT TOOK WELL over an hour to write up the report and Corcoran figured it would be best if the sheriff gathered all the jewelry and other items. It was coming time for him to take a short ride to the Chinese cemetery for his meeting with Donald Ferguson. He left the key to Moran's room on top of the report.

I'll be able to put a strong handcuff on Lathrop, he thought and chuckled at his own little joke. *I'll enjoy watching that man hang.* He walked to the courthouse stables and saddled Rube for the ride to the cemetery. *Locatelli will have to find out the various towns and cities that fool has been to recently to see if any of that loot is stolen.* He sat tall in the saddle and said right out to the cold night, "Or just sell it and keep most of the money, turning some in to the county."

It was a short ride in the middle of a cold night and Corcoran's mind was alive with thoughts of hanging Lathrop, stopping a major robbery, and solving the murder of Claire Donnegan. *No. I haven't solved that murder. Lathrop has but one arm. He couldn't possibly have killed Claire. She fought off her attacker, and surely would have beat the hell out of Lathrop. Somebody else killed Claire, he ended up with the necklace and sold it to Moran. I have to capture Lathrop alive.*

He was riding slow through the Chinese cemetery located at the deep end of a mine waste dump and saw Ferguson emerge from behind some pine trees. "Morning, Donald. Fancy meeting you here."

"Heard rumors about you and some jewelry salesman and wondered if you would be able to make it. Glad you're here, Corcoran. You sounded worried when you suggested this meeting." The undercover Wells

Fargo security agent wasn't dressed in a three-piece business suit, he wore canvas pants, rough wool shirt, and a heavy bearskin long coat.

"You look like you're going hunting, Ferguson."

"Man hunting, Terrence."

Corcoran chuckled thinking that he too would be man hunting, Lathrop hunting, when this meeting was over. "I heard a rumor that Jaeckes was building something north of town and took a little trip. I'm walking around without any backup, Ferguson and decided that I could use the services of the Johnson brothers." That brought a guffaw from Ferguson.

"Those boys aren't backup, Terrence, they're an entire skirmish line."

"I was at Washington's cabin when we saw Jaeckes and several men ride down the Lousetown Road. I followed them and found what Jaeckes has been building. It ain't a building, it's two mines with the entrance tunnels, the adits, extra wide." He paused to let that sink in, knowing Ferguson would pick up on the meaning immediately.

"They won't try to leave town, Corcoran. Just take a little fast ride north and hide the wagons." Ferguson was shaking his head, thinking about everything that could be done during and after the robbery attempt. "Diabolic," he chuckled. "If they did it right, our posse would think they went down Six Mile Canyon and they'd be safe. I have to get this word to my chief in Carson City."

"I put together a message yesterday and gave it to Sam Owens to get to U.S. Marshal McBride, outlining what I found out."

"Between Agent Murray and Marshal McBride, a

plan will be created.," Ferguson said. "Probably stop the robbery in its tracks at the depot, but if that should fail, have a posse waiting for the bastards at their own mine."

"That would work for me," Corcoran said.

"If they got all that gold tucked away underground, then what?" Ferguson asked.

"My guess is, they would pay off or kill those that worked for them, and then slowly move the gold to safe places a long way from the Comstock." Corcoran was shaking his head, reminding himself just how stupid the entire robbery would be. "I'm sure, Ferguson, that they would be better off simply taking a few hundred pounds and running hell for leather out of the territory."

Ferguson nodded with a smile, thinking the same thing. "Now, Mr. Corcoran sir, tell me about this jewelry salesman you arrested."

"I will, but how did you hear about that? It was well after midnight when that happened."

"I stopped for a brandy at the Washoe Club, and the place was buzzing about your big collar. They said blood was everywhere, the man was crying, and you beat him with every step to the courthouse."

"Maybe I should have, but I didn't." Corcoran took the next several minutes to tell Ferguson the whole story. Just the facts. He wrapped it up saying that he was going to tear Virginia City apart until he found Lathrop.

"Wouldn't want to be that man when you find him," Ferguson said. "Keep me posted on anything you get from McBride or hear from town folk, and I'll do the same. I better go get ready to be the district attorney's assistant," he chortled. The sky was just starting to lighten some and the intense cold seemed to get a bit more intense.

"LOOKS like you might have earned your pay last night, Corcoran. About time." Sheriff Locatelli was reading the report Corcoran left on top of the desk. "Word in town is you beat him up pretty bad."

"I hit him once when he made a fool move on me. I've spent the last few hours looking for Lathrop, but haven't found him yet. You better get with McNabb and get a warrant out before he skips town. The last time I saw him, he was with Jaeckes and Duffy. There's another pair to draw to."

"I'm getting mighty tired of hearing that name Jaeckes. I'll put our own warrant out on Lathrop. To hell with McNabb and his high falutin' ways. You look like hell, Corcoran. Go get some sleep."

"You don't have to tell me twice," Corcoran chuckled and headed out the door and the short walk to his new home at Jeb Miner's. The sun was up, streaming bright rays up Six Mile Canyon, across the top of Sugar Loaf peak, and warming the air. *I love that view. From where I'm standing I can see the Carson River, I can see Susan's Bluff, and I can pinpoint Fort Churchill. A man could live on visions like this.*

Visions of Orin Lathrop dangling from the end of a rope helped get the big man to sleep. He slept fully clothed, only managing to get his boots off before falling across the bed. It was late in the afternoon when he came back to life, at the prodding of Jeb Miner.

"What do you want? I just got here. Go away,"

Corcoran was tangled up in a wool blanket fighting off the efforts of Miner to get him up.

"It's three o'clock, Terrence. Time to go to work old man." Miner stepped back from a wild roundhouse right that missed by a mile and chuckled at the big deputy. "Tough guy, eh?" He laughed watching Corcoran slowly come around.

"Longest two days of my life, Jeb," he said. He found his boots, got the blanket squared away on the bed, and ran his fingers through unruly hair. "Three o'clock? What happened to a good old ten-hour shift? Just rattle some doors, say goodnight to the good folk, and sleep long and often?"

"You might want to know that no one has seen Boyington, Lathrop, or Duffy for at least two days." Miner and Corcoran found their way to the kitchen and Miner poured two cups of boiling coffee. "Also, it seems that a couple of women have reported missing jewelry. That was fast work, capturing Moran."

"He captured himself letting me see the necklace that I bought for Claire. He told me he bought it from Lathrop, but described the man, didn't call him by name. I'm thinking Lathrop might be a fence. Someone else killed Claire and stole the necklace, then sold it to Lathrop. He's still suffering from having his arm amputated and she would have beat the other arm off.

"I'm thinking that someone may be a burglar, disturbed Claire and she attacked him and died because of it. The first name that comes to mind is Clarence Boyington. I'll also wager, my fine friend, that I can find Boyington, Lathrop, and Duffy out on the plains near Lousetown."

Miner stood with a coffee cup in hand and a blank look on his face, took a drink of the hot stuff and shook his head. "Now, Terrence, why would they be out near Lousetown?

"Sit down, my friend, and let me tell you a story," Corcoran quipped. He spent the next half hour bringing the man up to speed on developments in the Wells Fargo delivery conspiracy. Once again, he left Donald Ferguson out of the story, and once again he would not be able to tell you why.

"That's absolutely amazing," Miner said when Corcoran finished. "You've been a busy boy."

Corcoran put his empty coffee cup down, strapped that hog-leg tight and headed out the door for another long all-night shift keeping Virginia City safe.

CHAPTER 14

WIND WHIPPED DOWN C STREET FROM THE NORTH, flinging dirt and debris in every direction, and Corcoran was wrapped tight in his buffalo robe long coat. He had a wool scarf wrapped around half his face and his old floppy sombrero pulled all the way down to his frozen ears. "I see we're blessed with a Washoe Zephyr," he snarled. "Next will come two feet of snow."

He stopped at Mollinelli's and said hello to Emil Rathburn and learned that Ike Smithson hadn't been seen for two days either. *It looks like Jaeckes is keeping his little gang together and out of sight. Maybe it's time for Washington Johnson to do a little on-site investigating.*

He made his way to D Street, found Skipper Johnson and made the suggestion. "You got that boy all fired up, Terrence. He's calling himself Corcoran's deputy. I'll get the word to him. Good work on that jewelry thief. Is that the man that killed Miss Claire?"

"Just lucky, Skipper. He didn't kill Claire, but he bought that necklace from Lathrop, and Lathrop got it from the man who killed that beautiful lady." Corcoran felt the anger building just talking about the murder. "Keep me posted. I think that shipment might be headed our way sometime in the next few days. The bank likes to be ready with money for the miners and there hasn't been a shipment for several weeks, according to Sam Owens. You have plenty of shells for that shotgun of yours?"

"Always," is all Skipper Johnson said.

"EVENING MICHAEL. I see the wind gods are blessing us tonight. Just plain coffee for right now, but keep that brandy bottle handy, it'll be a long shift again. Anything going on that I should know about?" Leaving Johnson's little shack, Corcoran was almost blown off Union Street as he made his way back up to C Street.

"Looks like that building next to the Bucket of Blood saloon might be sold. Three men from Denver arrived on the train this afternoon. They're planning another gambling parlor, saloon, and dance hall, as if we don't already have any. They don't look like business men, they look like killers."

These are going to be the big guns for Jaeckes and McNabb. I wondered when they might arrive. No way Tin Cup, Boyington, and Lathrop could handle that job. "Didn't happen to get any names, did you?" Corcoran figured there would be more than just three, but then again, he argued with himself, if you add McNabb's and Jaeckes' guns, there would be five professionals to go with Duffy's three idiots.

"They didn't come in here," Donahue said. "I saw them swagger into the Bucket and then heard the rumors of the possible sale. They might have been nicely dressed but they were carrying heavy iron."

"Maybe I better have a sip of that brandy, Michael, lad." He let the fire from the brandy burn its way down and pulled back into his heavy winter coat. "Keep the home fires burning, laddy buck, I'll be back."

He crossed to the west side of the street and tried the doors of the Bank of California, another business or two, and found himself pulling the heavy doors of the Washoe Club open. Jeb Miner caught his eye and nodded toward three men standing at the far end of the long bar.

Corcoran walked the length of the bar, said hello to a couple of men, and stood near the faro table, giving the impression that he was watching the game. There was a mirror slightly canted near the end of the bar that gave him a full view of the three strangers. *If these men are planning another saloon and gaming palace, it will be a rowdy one full of nasty people. Bad Sam Brown would be comfortable there, along with that fast knife of his, if he wasn't already dead.*

He watched the game for a few minutes and turned back down the bar, stopping about half way to get a cold beer. "Well, Jeb, it looks like McNabb has his troops on call."

"That's what I figured. That's Lefty Smith, James Suarez, and Harold Dolan. Smith's on the run from killing a Texas Ranger, Poncho Suarez is probably wanted in half a dozen states and territories, and Dolan is straight out of Chicago."

"Sounds like you've done your homework old man. I think I'll spend a little time at the International Hotel tonight and watch the action. I kept my coat on so they wouldn't spot the badge. I'll be a little more obvious at the hotel." He finished his drink and stood up. "First some supper with the lovely Suzanna O'Meara." He could hear Miner chuckling all the way out the door.

He was in the next block north when he spotted Daniel McKenzie trying to hide in the shadows near one of the markets. "McKenzie, stop where you are," Corcoran shouted, bounding into the street and running toward the man. McKenzie darted into the shadows and ran down the narrow strip between the buildings and out onto D Street where he had a horse tethered.

He was mounted and spurring the animal as Corcoran emerged from the shadows. Corcoran stopped, pulled that Peacemaker and took a long slow aim at the rider galloping down the street. The Colt Barked and McKenzie let out a howl of pain and fell from the animal. Corcoran took his time walking up to the downed man, writing in pain in the rocks and gravel of the street.

"So, Mr. McKenzie, I see you didn't leave town after all. Bet you wish you had," Corcoran chuckled, roughing the man to his feet. Let's get you tucked into jail and see if we can't find a doctor to tear that mean old bullet out of you."

IT WAS WELL after midnight when Corcoran finally arrived at the International Hotel. *Twenty-four hours ago, I made quite a scene here. No repeat performances, please.* He chuckled slipping out of his big coat and checking it with the lobby clerk. He was wearing brown canvas pants, a heavy red wool shirt, and black leather vest that displayed a shiny tin star. He made a slow round of the main floor saloon and gambling tables, sidled up to the bar and asked for a cup of coffee.

"Looks like you've got a busy night, Mr. Ainsworth. I need a full pot of your coffee, my friend." He had a miserable time getting McKenzie up to the courthouse and listening to all the whimpering. "Where'd all these people come from?"

"With the zephyr howling, no one wants to go home," the elderly barman laughed. "I got to see some of that jewelry and gold that man had that you arrested last night. My goodness it was pretty." He was polishing a glass for the second time and Corcoran thought there might just be something else the man had in mind.

"It was that," Corcoran answered. "Did you talk to that Moran fool?"

"Before you came in last night, he asked me to send Lathrop up to his suite if he came in. Didn't know Lathrop's name, just called him the man with one arm."

"Interesting." One thing every lawman has known from the time of the first lawman, if you want to know what's going on, ask your friendly local bartender. Old man Ainsworth has been behind the oak slab for more years than Corcoran has been alive, he was thinking. *If this old man doesn't know what's going on, no one in town does.*

"What do you know about Lathrop. I've had several run-ins with the man over the years. Never thought of him as a burglar, though." Corcoran watched the three Denver businessmen walk into the lounge from one of the gaming rooms in the mirror behind Ainsworth's head.

"He's not," the barman said. "He's a strong-arm thief and killer, or was before he lost that arm. No, it's Boyington who's the burglar. Since he lost his arm, Lathrop has been buying just about anything that Boyington steals and is selling it in Reno and Carson City."

"Most interesting, Mr. Ainsworth," Corcoran said. He slipped a small gold coin across the bar, indicated he could use another cup of coffee, and turned to watch the three men take seats at a table near the stage. The piano man was banging out some familiar old tunes and a couple of women were trying their best to sing the songs and dance to the out of time music.

"What are you lookin' at lawdog?" Lefty Smith snarled the question and his two companions turned to stare at Corcoran.

"Not much, I'd say," Corcoran quipped.

Smith growled something, stood up and started to walk toward where the deputy was standing. Hal Dolan stood up and blocked his way. "No, Lefty. No trouble. Remember? Now sit down and be quiet."

"Don't be pushin' me around Dolan. Who the hell made you the boss?"

"Maybe I did," Dolan answered. He did everything he could to keep his voice down, to not be heard by anyone else. "Think about the money, Lefty. Don't cause a ruckus. You know what McNabb said, and what Jaeckes said this afternoon. Enough money to set us up for the rest of our lives.

"Now, sit down, enjoy your drink, and be quiet."

Lefty Smith, eyes boring into Corcoran, growled again, turned his stare to Dolan, and slowly sank back into his chair. Corcoran chuckled loud enough to be heard and Smith jumped back up, turning the table over, and whipped his revolver out. Corcoran was faster because he instigated the play.

Smith's shot went into the floor at his feet, Corcoran's two shots went into Smith. The first one ripped into his shoulder and the second, an instant later, tore through his midsection, doing incredible damage. Smith staggered back, blood pouring from the two wounds, bounced off the stage, and went face down on the floor.

The large, exquisitely decorated barroom was hushed, men in silk suits, white ties and tails, quietly lit cigars, pulled money from tables, emptied glasses and gave serious thought to leaving the scene.

Corcoran stood still, the big forty-five at the ready, smoke curling from its hot steel barrel. The big deputy looked hard at the other two men. "That was very stupid of your friend," he said. "Don't make this worse, gentlemen."

"You had no call to kill him, sheriff," Dolan said. He was standing, facing Corcoran, his hand very close to the butt of his big iron. "You just killed our friend in cold blood."

"No," Corcoran said, long and slow. "I just killed a man who tried to kill me. Now, Mr. Dolan is it, I want you to use a finger and thumb and slowly pull that hog leg out and drop it on the floor."

"Won't do that, sheriff. You killed my friend in cold blood. You're going to die," and he went for it, diving to the side as he did. Dolan's only shot whisked past

Corcoran's head and killed the barman Ainsworth. Corcoran's two shots killed Dolan. One shot through his chest, on through his hip.

"I have two bullets left, Poncho," Corcoran said. He stood with his legs slightly spread, the revolver cocked and pointed at Suarez's chest. "Very slowly lift that piece from its leather and drop it on the floor. Then, equally slowly pull that monster knife and drop it too."

He watched Poncho Suarez carefully pull his revolver and drop it, then lift a beautiful knife with an elk-horn handle, and drop it. Corcoran nodded to the International Hotel security team that showed up. "If you gentlemen would be kind enough to gather those weapons and notify the mortuary, I would appreciate it. Please have those weapons brought to the courthouse, when you're done."

He turned to the third gunman, still standing near the overturned table. "Now, Mr. Suarez I want you to walk out that door, turn to the right, and walk up Union Street to the courthouse. I'll be five feet behind you, and sir, I want very much to kill you. Please give me a reason to do so."

The lobby clerk helped Corcoran into his heavy coat and Terrence walked another man to jail. *Keep this up and they won't let me back in that hotel. Poor Mr. Ainsworth. Damn fool just stood there behind me. Must have been scared helpless. I've told Locatelli a hundred times or more that we need more men on the street late at night. He has three or four deputies wandering around all day and lets me hang out alone all night. Damn.*

"So, Mr. Suarez, what exactly was that all about? I was led to believe you men were here in town to do some business. Trying to kill a deputy sheriff in front of twenty-five or more people isn't very smart. Who hired you?"

Suarez had his feet in leg-irons and was chained to the chair, his hands behind his back and cuffed, and was glowering at Corcoran. "You're a dead man, deputy," is all he said, in a heavy accent.

"We'll see." Corcoran unwrapped and unlocked the chains and stood the man up. "Just can't be nice to some people." He drove his right fist into Poncho's groin getting a full stomach eruption as the man howled and fell face first to the floor. "Now, once again, señor, who hired you?" There was only some groaning and Corcoran used the toe of his boot to nudge an answer. Actually, he stomped that toe into a set of ribs that gave way, and said again, "Who hired you?"

He had his report written and fresh coffee made by the time the sheriff arrived. There was one detail from the report that didn't get written and wouldn't until Corcoran figured out how he would play it.

"What the hell, Corcoran, three men tried to jump you, one at a time? Why? And old man Ainsworth is dead? Sumbitch, Terrence." Sheriff Emilio Locatelli sat at his desk, the report in front of him, shaking his head. "Those that saw all this agree that they started the problem? What do you do, just wander around at night shooting people? Two dead gunmen and one shot-up Miner's Union feller. Anyone I miss?"

"It's all in the report. Names, witnesses, and times. I went through your flyer file and found all the wanted posters. Smith, Dolan, and Suarez. Texas will be glad to hear about old Lefty Smith going down, and Dolan has papers all across the country. You might want to let the doc know that Suarez broke some ribs getting himself in jail."

"Go home and get some sleep, Corcoran." Terrence couldn't read minds, but if he could he would know that Locatelli was saying something to the effect that McNabb would not appreciate what he would tell him a bit later in the morning. "You weren't hurt at all?" He wanted to finish that statement with the word, damn.

CORCORAN DROPPED off an envelope at the Wells Fargo office addressed to Sam Owens before heading up to Miner's home on B Street. "This should slow Mr. McNabb and the duke down some. Their big guns weren't very big," and he snickered all the way up Taylor Street. *Suarez used both names, McNabb and Jaeckes, when he finally told me who hired him. Apparently, they were only told it was a large heist but no details. He never mentioned Locatelli, and yet I feel somehow the sheriff is involved in this mess. Why else has he not mentioned the rumors one time since I got back to town.*

He had to laugh when he muttered, "Everyone else in town is talking about it."

It was later in the day that U.S. Marshal McBride received that second envelope from Corcoran. He called his chief deputy into the office. "Look at this, Tom," he said, handing the sheet of paper over. "Corcoran took out two gunmen and has a third in custody. You'll be interested in the names."

Deputy U.S. Marshal Thomas Simpson, thirty-years-old and a veteran of more than ten years' service, took the letter and sat down across from McBride. "They'll be dancing in the streets when those Texas Rangers hear that Lefty Smith is dead. Corcoran took out Hal Dolan, too? Glad he's on our side, Marshal."

McBride chuckled some and took the note back. "We now know about the mines or tunnels north of Virginia City, and we know that it is McNabb and Jaeckes who are doing the planning. Now, they don't have any hired guns, so I wonder if their plans are on hold, or if they're going to try for the shipment with those few fools Corcoran describes?"

"Personally, Marshal, I think we should continue on as if the robbery is going to take place. If they don't make the attempt, we're not out anything, and if they do, we'll be in a position to end it immediately."

"I agree, Tom. Get with Parks and put your teams together. That shipment will be going up day after tomorrow, according to Wells Fargo. The mint will have everything crated and ready tomorrow night. Each crate will weigh two hundred pounds, so it will take two men to move them."

"I'm sure Jaeckes will wait until the crates are moved from the railcar onto the wagons before he strikes." Simpson knew the area around the railroad's freight depot in Virginia City well. "I'd like to have at least five deputies with me at the depot. With Wells Fargo security people on hand also, that should be more than enough fire-power."

"We'll need mounted men near the Lousetown road as well, Tom. If one or more of those wagons should break loose, we need to stop them before they can hide the wagons in the mines. Corcoran says the mine entrances would be easily defended and we don't want to get into a prolonged fire-fight if we don't have to."

"Did you read Corcoran's description of the Johnson brothers? I'll have three deputies assigned to work with them." He was laughing, thinking about Skipper and Washington Johnson ready to take on Jaeckes' gang. "I'm looking forward to meeting those two."

The two talked for another few minutes and Simpson left to find Deputy U.S. Marshal Emil Parks and work out the details. McBride wrote a note to be sent back to the Wells Fargo clerk in Virginia City for Corcoran.

"This is the highest security, Parks," Simpson said. "I want at least eight men besides you and me on this detail. You and three men, mounted, waiting at the Johnson cabin on the Lousetown Road, and I with five men at the depot in Virginia City. I want to meet with all of you this evening."

"Got it Tom," Parks said. "I'll have to draw from the mint security team for two bodies, but they are fine lawmen in their own right. What did McBride have to say?"

"Only that several of the big guns we might have been facing were taken out by a Virginia City deputy, so we'll probably only be facing local criminals, not hired killers. That is, if the plan actually takes place."

CHAPTER 15

SAM OWENS WAS BANGING ON THE FRONT DOOR OF JEB Miner's home just before noon, getting both Miner and Corcoran out of bed. "What the hell's all the noise?" Miner said, getting the front door opened.

"Gotta see Corcoran," Owens stammered. He had run from the Wells Fargo offices up steep Taylor Street to Miner's place. "It's very important."

Corcoran came out of his veil of darkness, fumbled for boots and pants, and stumbled into the front parlor. "Sam. Something important?" *Of course, it's something important, fool. Will I ever get a full serving of sleep?* "Okay, Sam, calm down now and tell me what's going on."

"Here, Terrence. From Marshal McBride. Also, my people in Carson City say the shipment will be on the morning express. I'm arranging for the teams and wagons now."

Corcoran took the envelope from Owens, saw that McBride had scrawled IMPORTANT across the front, and opened it up. "Looks like it's time to go to work," he said. "The mint will be loading the Wells Fargo railcar tonight and the train will be here in the morning. Jeb, are you up to working as part of the security?" Corcoran had his plan put together days ago and now just needed to make sure all the people were ready to fill their places. In his mind, the only things he couldn't control were the outlaws themselves.

He knew where the wagons had to be and knew where the security force had to be to keep those wagons from ever leaving the route between the depot and the bank. Exactly where and when the outlaws would make their strike was the missing part.

"I can't run, Terrence, and I doubt I'd be much good in a fight. My arms and shoulders are still pretty much screwed up by those rocks. I could be a good lookout, though."

"That'll work. If they do break out, it's important we know where they go. I'm sure they'll head for the Lousetown tunnels, but if you were at that point where they could turn down Six Mile Canyon instead, you would be able to direct the posse." Corcoran figured they would drive the teams north from the depot and could turn east and down Six Mile Canyon at Mill Street, if they wanted, or continue straight north to Lousetown.

"I'll set myself up first thing in the morning, Terrence. What do you think Locatelli's gonna do?"

"I know he and McNabb will try to keep me as far away as possible. I've already alerted McBride to that. I'll be with Skipper and Washington out at their cabin. According to this note, I'll have three or four marshals out there with us." The group moved into Jeb Miner's large kitchen and was standing around the wood stove waiting for the coffee to boil.

On the road north there was one other spot that bothered Corcoran. "Where the Seven Mile Canyon road joins the Lousetown trail," he murmured. "They could turn east there, too, and end up on the Six Mile Canyon road. I'll need to put someone there." He poured coffee for everyone.

"Sam, you better get hustling. Make sure you say nothing about any of this to either Locatelli or McNabb. That express will be here at eight tomorrow morning so I'll do some of my regular rounds tonight and then head out to the Johnson's cabin. Jeb, you'll want to be in position before eight o'clock, and Sam, just do your regular duties and stay out of the line of fire."

Finding out about those tunnels is the key to this operation. If I hadn't stumbled onto them we'd be setting up to stop this gang of idiots on roads all over town. McNabb and Jaeckes have a good plan for hiding the loot but are really being stupid on where they plan to make the heist. Should have derailed the train after coming through one of the tunnels before American Flats.

He was still chuckling to himself as he finished dressing for his shift. *Here I am planning to stop this big old robbery and at the same time planning on where they should have made the robbery.*

"EVENING SHERIFF," Corcoran said. "Looks like that new

storm fell apart on us, eh? It's gonna be a cold night, though."

"Yeah. Look, Corcoran, McNabb says he's had three reports of possible cattle thefts from some of the ranchers down near Sutro. Make a round of town and then take a ride down there, will you? And get reports from the ranchers."

"That's not even in our jurisdiction, sheriff. What would I do?" *Well, now. That's one way to get me out of town. Send me ten miles east, into another county, and talk to ranchers about how nice it will be when spring gets here. Nice try, Locatelli.*

"I know, but McNabb says we are doing a favor by looking into this. Let's not ruffle his feathers too much." Locatelli looked like he had eaten a mouthful of feathers, like he didn't want to do what he just did, but was working on orders. Corcoran just smiled and agreed to make the ride.

McNabb has something on Locatelli. The sheriff may or may not be involved in this heist, but he's being used by McNabb. Locatelli never talks about his life, current or past, but McNabb knows something and he's using it. Corcoran was one of those people who never turned their minds off and he knew that for whatever time it took, he would figure out what McNabb knew.

The big deputy poured a mug of boiling coffee and settled down in a cane chair across from the sheriff. "Did you get any witness statements on last night's little problem at the hotel?"

"Everyone said basically what your report said. I sent wires to Texas and to some of the places where Harold Dolan was wanted. You'll have some reward money coming in, I think." While the news brought a smile to Corcoran's mug, he was more interested in whether Locatelli had pressed Suarez and if the Mexican had talked about the upcoming Wells Fargo robbery.

"Did you get anything more out of Suarez? As soon as Smith saw me, I knew it was going to be a fight. Don't for the life of me know why, though." Corcoran played dumb to see if the sheriff would say something, give something away, but he just indicated that Suarez wasn't talking.

"You hurt him bad, Terrence. The doc moved him down to the hospital. I've got him chained to his bed, and the doc didn't like that either. You won't get back from Sutro before I come in tomorrow, so just go on home when you do get back. Don't worry about checking in with me."

Sure, sheriff, that way maybe I won't even find out about the big robbery until sometime late tomorrow. You're doing a good job for your boss McNabb. I'm going to take both you bums down and out, and very soon. The duke of velvet too. Corcoran pulled his heavy coat on and left the office, with one stop across the hall to say hello to Donald Ferguson.

"Evening, Mr. Ferguson. Looks like we get a break in the weather tonight."

"I think so, Terrence," he said. He gently slipped a folded piece of paper to the edge of the desk and Corcoran leaned on the desk, palming the paper. "That was quite a mess you got into last night. Those men were wanted in all four corners of the compass, I think." Ferguson leaned toward Corcoran and whispered, "Mr. McNabb has already left the office, but he wants statements from you. He's one angry little man," Ferguson chuckled.

"I'll just bet he is," Corcoran whispered back. "I better hit the streets and keep our town safe from the rowdies. Have a good night, Mr. Ferguson." He walked out onto B Street and turned north, intending to make a sweep through the International Hotel before touring C Street. Inside, he stopped at the bar and ordered a cup of coffee before opening the folded paper Ferguson gave him.

It was a somber scene, with employees mourning the loss of the long-time barman, and having to clean of the mess that Corcoran left them. The deputy got weak smiles from some of the employees, and downright glares from others. *I raised hell two nights in a row in here. I guess some of them have a right to be a bit upset.*

"So, everything is in place," he murmured. "Many of the marshals will be in the Wells Fargo railcar, others may already be in town, and those I'll be with are probably moving toward the Johnson cabin." He noticed many eyes trying not to make contact with his and wondered if they thought he came to raise more hell in their splendid digs.

He drank his coffee, walked through one of the gaming rooms, nodded to the dealers and players that would look at him, smiled often, and made his way out the massive front entrance onto C Street. He rattled doors heading south, greeting people, scowling at some of the low-life out early in the evening, and made his way to the Sazerac Club.

Many of the businesses were closing for the day and there were still many people out and about. After the past two days, Corcoran found himself answering lots of questions, about jewel thefts, about hired gunslingers, and always about when the next storm would arrive.

"Michael Donahue, it's a good evening to you," he said, pulling out of his coat. "I think a hot brandy would just about set me up for a long shift on a cold night. What did I miss during this fine day?"

"Up and down these streets made from pure silver, the word is that we're lucky to live in a community with a lawman like Terrence Corcoran to shoot up the bad guys." He was laughing and slapping his hands, doing a little dance imitating pulling a gun and shooting it off. His comment about the streets had to do with the fact that a lot of the less than desirable crushed rock from some of the mines was used on the streets as gravel. It did contain some silver according to many of those that did the mining.

"If they liked today, just wait until tomorrow my Irish brother," Corcoran quipped. "It's going down." He took a long drink of the brandy. "You might want to stay off the streets near the depot when the express comes in. Have you seen the likes of Tin Cup, Lathrop, Boyington, or Smithson? I doubt they're in town, but with those fools, you never know."

"Haven't seen them for days, now that you bring it up. What's the word from Jaeckes? He must be furious after your antics last night."

"Haven't seen him or McNabb. They're probably having Hungarian tea in Jaeckes' suite right about now, trying to figure out if tomorrow will actually take place. I better make my rounds, Michael. Not a word about this. I won't be back tonight, so don't worry if you don't see me."

With Donahue's background, Corcoran knew his words were safe and Donahue gave him a good nod. "Wish I was just a wee bit younger, Terrence. I'd love to join your little party, but I don't think these old bones would back me up."

Corcoran made his way across the street to the Washoe Club so that he would be seen, and planned on leaving there and riding out to the Johnson cabin. He wanted to make sure that he was seen leaving town, just in case the sheriff had eyes out for him. He was certain that either Locatelli or McNabb would have someone watching his every move.

If Locatelli questioned Suarez I wonder if Suarez told him anything? I wonder if McNabb and company are aware that I know everything. If so, they could be making other plans or rewriting what they have. "Well, ain't nothing I can do about that," he muttered, making his way down C Street. The night had turned bitter cold with a north wind kicking up everything that wasn't firmly attached to something.

"Maybe on top of everything else, we'll have a blue norther drop in on us for tomorrow's big show." He was almost laughing, pushing his way against the gusts.

"WE SHOULD HAVE HAD that man killed the minute he arrived back in town," McNabb said, pacing around the lovely suite in the International Hotel. "This is bad, Jaeckes. Very bad. Those men were the best that money could buy and we don't have time to try to replace them.

"Should we cancel our plans? My God, Jaeckes, I can't imagine not getting my hands on that gold. Thousands and thousands of dollars is about to be ours, and I won't let it get away. We've been planning this for more than a year and one big damn deputy isn't going to deny me what I want." He was in a rage, his pacing getting faster with each turn around the suite. "He simply shot Lefty Smith and Harold Dolan in cold blood, and beat the hell out of Poncho Suarez."

"I've talked with Duffy and Boyington, Ezra," Jaeckes said. "They agree that we should go ahead with our plans. Smithson is very good with a gun, Lathrop has been practicing his left-hand shooting every day and is good, and we know that Duffy and Boyington are good.

"I've hired three men to drive the teams so that our men are free to use their guns. That fool at the livery just went along with who I said would be driving. We must go through with this." Jaeckes' head was as filled with visions of thousands of gold coins as the district attorney's and the two could only see themselves living in some paradise somewhere across a broad ocean.

"We'll have to get rid of those three drivers, though. I'm not willing to pay them or give them a split. They aren't actually part of this deal," Jaeckes said.

"I had the sheriff send Corcoran out of town, so at least he won't be around. We'll have to fight off the Wells Fargo security people, and that's about it. Sometimes they send a deputy U.S. Marshal along, but we'll only be facing about four guns at the most.

"We were planning to not be with Hal Dolan and all

of them, but with those men dead or in jail, I think we must be there, Jaeckes. Our guns might be needed."

"I was already planning on it, McNabb. I want to be on the lead wagon and you should be also. I'm going to have M'Toobie driving that wagon and carrying that monster shotgun of his."

"That's good. I'll see you at the stables at seven tomorrow morning." McNabb drained his drink, slipped into his coat and left the suite for the short walk to his home on B Street. Jaeckes went to bed immediately, planning on dreams filled with a ton or more of gold coins twinkling in stardust.

DEPUTY U.S. MARSHAL Tony Simpson hadn't shaved in three days, was wearing buckaroo regalia and had his badge in his pocket instead of pinned to his coat. He and two other men, dressed as working cattlemen, rode into Virginia City about six o'clock in the morning, leaving their horses tied close to the railroad depot. "Let's get some coffee and talk to the clerk," Simpson said.

"Good morning, gentlemen," the man behind the counter said. "What can I do for you?"

"We'll be taking the train to Carson City, then on to Elko, if you'll sell us some tickets and get us a good strong cup of coffee, sir." Simpson didn't recognize the clerk and wondered if there had been changes made that he wasn't aware of. The clerk should have been a marshal.

"I'll get the coffee then work on those tickets," the clerk said, walking to a wood stove at the back of his little office. He brought three mugs of coffee out and when he set them down he let his coat open enough for Simpson to see the badge. "I'm mint security," he whispered, closing the coat back. "Enjoy your coffee. It'll take a few minutes to get these tickets set up."

Simpson smiled and sipped his coffee. "Make sure you include our horses on those tickets, please. Got a good job waiting for us in Elko. How long will the trip take?"

"It's a good four hundred miles out there, so plan on being on the train for some time. We'll provide food and water for your horses, but it is extra." This was just all talk for the benefit of anyone who might be listening. Those horses were there for the chase if it came to that.

Deputy U.S. Marshal Enid Parks and two deputies rode through Virginia City about three o'clock in the morning, heading north toward the Lousetown Road. Parks was raised on the Comstock and knew his way around the area as any kid would. He kept the group on the well-used roads and out of the residential areas so if they were seen it wouldn't be an anomaly.

"About another hour and we'll be at Johnson's cabin. I'm really looking forward to meeting those giant Johnson brothers," he chuckled. McBride had spread the word among his men that they would be working with Corcoran and the Johnsons, and described just how big those brothers were. "Corcoran's letter gave me the idea these guys are monsters."

It was an easy ride under a full moon and bright stars on a good road, and the men let their horses walk at their own speed. The wind was screaming its wrath, doing its best to unseat the men, but the clouds and snow were not to be seen, at least yet.

When they crossed the ridge, and dropped into the long valley they could see the Johnson cabin because of lamplight in a window. "Looks like they're waiting for us," Parks said. They were still a few of miles out and didn't increase their pace.

M'TOOBIE and two other men walked into the stables at seven o'clock. The liveryman was waiting for them, and they gathered the horses, got them harnessed and hitched within twenty minutes, and prepared for the short ride to the railroad depot. At fifteen minutes before eight o'clock, McNabb and Jaeckes walked into the barn.

Both men wore their side arms as a gunman would, and both carried double barrel shotguns as well. "M'Toobie, you drive the lead wagon. Mr. McNabb and I will ride with you. You," and he pointed at one of the new hired men, "drive the second wagon, and Tin Cup and Smithson, you ride with him. And you," he pointed at another man, "drive the third wagon, and Lathrop, you and Boyington ride with him.

"Any questions? Good, then mount up and let's get our hands on some of that gold."

"All of that gold," McNabb said.

They didn't notice that the three new men Jaeckes had hired to drive looked at each other, with big questions on their faces. Nobody said anything, but at least two of the men looked like they would bolt at the first shot.

The three wagons each with four up pulled up to the loading area just as the morning express rolled into the yard, belching smoke as it emerged from the tunnel just north of the ornate St. Mary of the Mountains Catholic church. The train spit steam, blasted its horn loud and long, and squealed to a stop.

CHAPTER 16

As Parks and his men rode onto the Johnson property, the door opened and Terrence Corcoran stepped onto the porch. "Nice morning for a little horseback ride, eh marshal? Put your horses around behind the cabin. There's a nice corral and they can't be seen from the main road. Any trouble coming through town?"

"Saw a couple of drunks staggering near the cribs and that's about it Corcoran," Parks said. He stepped off his horse and handed the reins to one of the deputies. The first vestiges of sunrise were giving a tint to some early morning mist over the eastern mountains. "Looks like we'll have fair weather for our hunt if those fools break free."

"You might call this fair weather, Corcoran, I call it North Pole cold," Parks said, burrowing even deeper into his heavy long coat. "You people who live at these high altitudes get used to it, I guess. Not for me." Corcoran chuckled along with the marshal.

"We call it a zephyr and laugh in its face," Corcoran said, ushering him into the cabin.

It was crowded in the Johnson cabin and the stove was keeping the rooms more than warm. The large coffee pot was boiling away as everyone introduced himself and Parks got down to business. "Just how the hell big are you, Mr. Johnson?" He stammered, walking around Washington Johnson, opening his arms wide to touch each of the man's shoulders, then standing back to back with the man, knowing his head was lower than Washington's. "Well," he laughed. "That was fun. Now down to business.

"Did you have some kind of plan in mind if Jaeckes and company break free?"

"I wanted to put two of us at the tunnels and the rest here to follow the gang when they rode through, but Washington says they have armed guards at the tunnels, so that's out. Right now, I'm thinking we just run 'em down. Those horses pulling heavy wagons will be pretty tired by the time they get here."

"We'll see their dust as soon as they clear that ridge," Washington Johnson said, "long's this wind keeps up." He pointed out the window toward the low ridge off in the distance. Parks stood alongside Corcoran and measured himself against Johnson. Parks was larger than Corcoran, heftier in the shoulders and chest and taller by an inch or two. He felt almost small standing there next to the black giant. He couldn't keep the grin off his face.

Washington Johnson's arms were the size of Parks' thighs, he saw, and those shoulders were more like boulders. The man had no neck. Where his shoulders left off his head began, and it was completely bald and shone like obsidian. Parks took a big gulp of air and simply said, "That's our play then." Corcoran had to chuckle fully understanding what was going through the deputy marshal's mind.

"That train's due in at eight, and if they do break free with a wagon load of gold and silver, we won't see any action for some time." Parks was standing at a window watching the day emerge from its slumber. "Let's get comfortable, maybe catch forty winks. Corcoran, why don't you take first watch." Bodies sprawled out on the floor and Terrence Corcoran stepped outside to watch more of the sunrise.

When this is all over, I'm gonna find a nice little ranch way up in the mountains somewhere and take out all my frustrations on poor helpless cows. Too many lives are all messed up because of all the gold and silver, all that greed, all that arrogance. I'll grab hol't of lovely Suzanna and ride for the high country. The sky exploded in twelve shades of red as the sun slowly made itself known and Corcoran kicked a rock, shoved his hands deeper into the pockets of that buffalo robe coat, smiled gently, and kicked another rock as he walked back into Johnson's cabin.

THE BIG DOORS on the Wells Fargo railcar rolled open and two men inside moved a crate up to the opening as a wagon pulled up. Jaeckes and McNabb, their floppy hats pulled down tight to hide their faces, stood in the back of the wagon and lifted the crates into place, one at a time. M'Toobie sat motionless on the driver's seat, his shotgun cradled but mostly out of sight.

Sheriff Locatelli was just riding up and tied his horse off with three others and sauntered toward the loading docks. Ike Smithson raised his rifle and was taking a long slow aim when a large man jerked the sheriff into the depot, whirled him around, and smashed a rifle butt into the back of his head. "Cuff him and hold him until this is all over," the deputy marshal said.

When the wagon was full a Wells Fargo man directed the wagon to a holding place to wait until the other two wagons were filled. One Wells Fargo security man with a shotgun stood near the wagon and another stood near the railcar. McNabb whispered to Jaeckes that they must not have any idea of the planned robbery if that's the security they brought.

The second and then the third wagons were filled and the two Wells Fargo security men mounted up and indicated the wagons should follow them to the Bank of California. Deputy U.S. Marshal Simpson and his men mounted their horses, tied next to the sheriff's, out of sight of the wagons and rode around the north end of the train, two deputy marshals inside the Wells Fargo railcar had their rifles aimed at the wagon drivers' heads.

At a nudge from Elon Jaeckes, M'Toobie smacked the team and howled for them to run, pulled the shotgun up to blast the agents who were in front. A rifle bullet between his shoulders ended that idea and he dropped the shotgun, almost dropped the reins, and slowly collapsed into the high seat's boot.

McNabb jumped across the seat and grabbed up the

reins, whipping the horses and yelling at them, getting them into a full gallop toward the Lousetown Road. Jaeckes heard rifle shots, heard bullets whipping the air close to his head as he dove into the crates of gold.

The two security agents had their rifles up and were firing at the drivers and passengers of the other two wagons, as were the deputy marshals inside the railcar. Tin Cup Duffy died instantly with a bullet through his head, Boyington was down with wounds to his legs and chest, Lathrop jumped out of the wagon and tried to run for cover only to be shot in the back twice.

Ike Smithson was the only smart one in the bunch. He threw his shotgun aside and put both hands in the air. The drivers of the wagons did not follow M'Toobie's wagon, and simply sat in their seats, the reins hanging loose in their hands. It was all over in less than one minute.

Simpson and his deputies came around from in front of the engine and took up the chase to catch Jaeckes and McNabb. The wagon was only about fifty yards or so in front of them. "Let's just keep them in sight, gentlemen," Simpson said, smiling through the dust. "At the speed McNabb is pushing those horses, and the weight they're pulling, they'll give out soon."

When the deputies neared the Six Mile Canyon junction, Jeb Miner stood up from a clump of sage and pointed north. Simpson waved a thank you, and at a steady lope they followed the wagon toward Lousetown. "They'll have to climb that steep little section in order to clear the ridge before dropping into Long Valley. There's no valid reason for any of us to get shot, boys, so let's not crowd them.

"When they drop into Long Valley they'll be met by Parks and that group, and we'll take 'em down. Those horses will be ruined by then." Simpson had his doubts that the horses would even last that long. At better than six thousand feet above sea-level, there just isn't that much oxygen in the air, and those horses were being driven much harder than they should be.

"Let's make sure they don't make hat big turn down toward Six Mile Canyon. If they do, we'll take them before they hit the big down grade." He got nods from each, they continued their comfortable lope on a bright but intensely cold morning. If anything, the wind was stronger than before sunrise.

"THEY WERE EXPECTING US, MCNABB," Jaeckes said, standing back up behind the driver's seat. "First Dolan's gunmen are gone and then this. We must save this gold." He was screaming into the wind, pounding on McNabb's back. McNabb reached around and slapped him hard.

"Shut up and think, you fool. Is anyone following us? Do they have a posse behind us? Get ready to shoot anyone that comes up from behind us." He was continuing to whip the horses and kept them in a full gallop on the rocky trail. "If you see anyone coming up behind us, don't hesitate, just shoot 'em."

The trail was narrow in most places, with run-off ditches that would spill water over the road during spring thaw. Because of the recent storms and strong winds, the ditches were filled with dirty snow and ice making it difficult to see the edge of the road. McNabb was not an experienced teamster and the four-up were being constantly whipped. They were approaching the most difficult part of their escape, making it up a steep section of road with worn out horses.

There were at least four switchbacks on the long climb and the horses were walking slowly despite the constant crack and snap of McNabb's whip. The switchbacks were hard enough to navigate by a working teamster, and McNabb had to back the wagon more than once, screaming obscenities at the horses.

Jaeckes was whimpering about saving his gold, but did get down behind one of the crates and took up a position giving him full view of the road behind them. He could see dust back down the trail a ways, but it was some way off. "I think we're being followed, McNabb, but they aren't trying to catch up with us."

McNabb saw Simpson's plan immediately, but kept right on urging those horses to go faster. "We have to clear that ridge," he said. "Clear that ridge and I can ease up on these horses. If we can make the tunnels we can hold them off, and get away late tonight." McNabb had already given up on the gold. In his mind, he would put a bag or two of double eagles in his saddlebags and ride with wind out of Washoe.

The road up to the ridge was steep and those hard switchbacks had slowed things to a crawl. The horses were faltering. One lead horse tripped and almost went down, which brought the team to an even slower walk. McNabb whipped them viciously, screaming at them, and they managed to get into a slow trot. The men behind were getting closer and Jaeckes howled at McNabb to get moving.

"Shoot the bastards," McNabb howled back. The horses were just walking and would not go any faster. They were a hundred yards from the crest of the ridge when the horses quit. The one leader that tripped simply collapsed in the middle of the trail. McNabb jumped from the wagon and darted into the sagebrush, running as fast as he could.

Simpson saw the horse go down and pulled up. He motioned to his men to spread out wide and move slowly up to the wagon. Neither Simpson nor any of the deputies saw McNabb jump down from the high wagon. As they moved closer, Jaeckes started shooting, but they were well out of range.

Simpson waved the deputies farther apart, making it impossible for Jaeckes to see all of them at the same time. They were in a great fan moving ever closer to the former Chicago gunman. "Let's move up nice and slow, men. When we start to get close to being in range, we'll dismount and using this brush as cover, close on the shooter."

They rode until they could see the bullets falling in front of them and dismounted, tying their horses to some brush. They slowly moved up on the wagon, Jaeckes firing at anything and everything, first left, then right, never really seeing a target. It was Simpson who moved within thirty yards or so of the wagon.

"You in the wagon. This is Deputy U.S. Marshal Tony Simpson. Throw your weapons out and stand up. You are surrounded. Give up and you'll live." Simpson nodded to his deputies to not shoot if Jaeckes gave up. "I'll only give you to the count of ten and then we'll kill you," Simpson shouted.

They watched as first a rifle and then a revolver was thrown out from behind one of the crates filled with gold. Elon Jaeckes slowly stood up, his hands high in the air. "Where's the driver?" Simpson yelled, and Jaeckes turned to see that McNabb had fled. He didn't say anything as the deputies jerked him off the wagon and threw him face down in the sand and rocks. A set of handcuffs, nice and tight were clamped on his wrists.

Simpson had two of the deputies look for the driver's prints in the surrounding sand, rotten snow, and dirt. "Looks like he hightailed it toward the crest, Tony. He stayed in the brush, not on the trail. Want us to follow"

"Make sure you know where he's going. We can pick him up after we secure this gold." The deputy followed the trail for fifteen minutes or so and then returned to the wagon.

"He's making his way down into Long Valley, I'm sure," the deputy said. "Probably end up at those tunnels in a couple of hours."

"We'll have to leave this one horse, I'm afraid," Simpson said. "He's done for. What a damn waste. Let's slowly move this wagon on across the ridge and down to Johnson's place. Henry, why don't you and Freddy escort our fine Hungarian duke back to Virginia City and Cletus and I will get the wagon down into Long Valley. Bring some help and a couple of teams, after you get Jaeckes settled."

THE COLD WAS GNAWING at that heavy buffalo robe long coat Corcoran was wearing and he stepped inside the cabin. "By my calculation, we should see something in the next half hour or so, Parks. Let's get everyone up and wide awake for whatever comes."

"Doesn't sound like the storm's let up at all," Parks said. "I'm glad to be here with all you fine folks but I surely wish I was at the depot."

"Knowing a little background on McNabb and Jaeckes, I think it's safe to say that we're gonna get our fair share of action before this is over. How many men did you say were guarding the tunnels, Washington?"

"I'm sure I counted four, Terrence. Of course, there could have been others inside that I couldn't see."

"Our best bet then if a wagon or more show up, is to take them down well before they get to the tunnels. No sense making it harder on ourselves. Check your weapons and let's keep a close watch on that ridge." Corcoran grabbed his trusty Winchester, opened the action and closed it, seeing a round at the ready. "I'm really looking forward to jamming this right up McNabb's nose," Corcoran laughed.

MCNABB WAS TUCKED down behind some rocks and watched all the action, not daring to move. All thoughts of the gold were gone and his only concern now was to get as far away from this place as he could. He watched Simpson unhitch the one horse that was down and was able to move it off the roadway. It took many minutes and both men to get it on its feet.

"He'll live, but he's ruined now. Let's see if these three can manage to get us down to Johnson's." He started to climb into the seat when he spotted M'Toobie's body in the bottom of the driver's area. "Cletus, come here. The driver didn't run away, he's dead. Must have been shot during the robbery. My God, he's big, like a giant."

"Whose tracks were we following? Somebody jumped off the wagon, Simpson. Are you sure you want to leave that horse?" Cletus was positive they had been following fresh tracks, and if that person should double back, he would have a horse. Maybe worn out, but a horse that could be ridden at a walk.

"He's helpless," Simpson said. "Tie your horse off and ride up here with me and let's get going."

McNabb waited until the wagon was over the crest and carefully walked up to the worn-out horse. *They left the halter on him but what would I do for reins?* He stripped his frock coat off and unbuttoned his suspenders, pulled a little cigar knife and separated them into equal length pieces. *This will at least get me to the tunnels.*

"Dust," is all Skipper Johnson said, pointing out toward the hillside. "They be moving mighty slow, Terrence." Parks walked out of the cabin to join the two and pulled a field telescope from his duster.

"Something's wrong," he muttered. He handed the scope to Corcoran. "Looked like only three horses in the rig, two men on the driver's seat, and trailing one horse."

"Yup, that's what I see. We better ride out there, Parks. I don't recognize either man on the wagon and surely if it's McNabb and Jaeckes they wouldn't be trailing a saddle horse."

It took the group less than fifteen minutes at a brisk lope to ride up to the gold-filled wagon. "So, Deputy Simpson, you've become a road agent, eh?" Parks was laughing, and then everything got very serious. Simpson spent the next several minutes telling about how the chase had ended.

"Did you shoot that worn out horse?" Corcoran knew that if the man they captured was Jaeckes, and it was certain the dead man was M'Toobie, then the man that got away almost had to be McNabb.

"No, of course not," Simpson said.

"The tracks that you saw would probably have been made by McNabb. That devious bastard probably back-tracked and is now riding that horse." He spat his anger in the dirt and mounted his horse. "Washington, can you help these fine gentlemen get their precious gold back to Virginia City?" Washington scowled but agreed.

"Skipper, let's you and me ride up to that ridge and find McNabb's trail. Damn," he said. *They're probably good with their weapons but those marshals need to spend some time out of the office. That was really stupid to leave that horse.*" As winded and worn out as it was, it would recover enough to be able to walk and if McNabb could get it to some water, within an hour or two, he would have a fair horse.

Corcoran and Skipper Johnson made good time back to the ridge crest and found where the horse had been led off into the sagebrush. Hoof prints and boot prints led through the brush and rocks and started down the north side of the hillside. "He'll head for those springs down there," Skipper Johnson said. He was pointing at a stand of cottonwood trees and green grass about a mile away, on the valley floor.

"He's leading the horse and letting it get its strength back. It's an easy trail to follow, Skipper, and I'm sure you're right about the springs. Let's ride straight for the springs and not worry about his trail."

They side hilled through rocky country in an almost straight line toward the springs. "I'm sure McNabb is well armed, Skipper, so let's not make good targets. Chances are he'll head for the tunnels as soon as the horse gets watered."

"Look at hose clouds, off to the northwest, Terrence. This little zephyr gonna be filled with snow and ice before too much longer."

McNabb was wearing regular lace up, high top shoes, not good boots, and it wasn't long that he started having foot problems. His ankle twisted more times that he could keep track of, and the soft leather allowed pointed and sharp rocks to gouge at his toes and feet. He was just a couple of hundred yards from the springs when he tripped over a sharp rock and fell in the grass.

"Damn it." He nursed a bleeding toe that showed through a rip in the thin shoe leather, got to his feet and made the last yards to water. He and the horse splashed into the water that fast. He stood up, drenched and dripping. Ice crystals were forming as he led the horse to some shade and grass. He wanted a fire more than anything and wondered where it was the marshals were taking the wagon load of gold. That's when he spotted

Corcoran and Johnson coming down the hillside, less than a quarter mile away.

McNabb jumped onto the draft horse, hoped his suspenders would really work for reins and nudged the big boy into a trot, away from imminent capture. The tunnels were less than seven miles away but he would be traveling cross-country, not on a trail, and the hillside wasn't just a straight line, either.

"I've got to move back down onto the valley floor to make the best time and if I do that, I'll be seen immediately." He decided to stay along the hillsides, using stands of pine and cedar for cover, moving over the humps and down into the shallow valleys, at a fast walk. His mind only told him to escape, to get to the tunnels where there would be help. With a belly full of good water and a few mouthfuls of fresh grass, the horse was willing to walk at a fast pace. McNabb couldn't get any more out of him than that.

He had ripped part of his shirt to tie around his hurt toe, but it fell off somewhere along the trail, and his foot was bleeding again. The shoe was a wet rag now and the toe was about twice the normal size.

WASHINGTON JOHNSON WOULD HAVE PREFERRED GOING with Corcoran and his brother, but did his best to get one of his horses into the extra harness and send the wagon and deputy marshals back toward Virginia City. Parks argued with Washington, but the huge man finally got his message across.

"Look, you heard Corcoran, and that man knows this country, McNabb will do everything he can to get back to those tunnels. Leave me one deputy and we can ride to the tunnels and be some help.

"I know you can't just ride off and leave all that gold, it has to get back to town, but all I need is one man. There are gunmen at those tunnels and Corcoran and Skipper will need help."

Washington Johnson was fierce looking and Parks wondered if he might get a bit physical if he didn't approve of leaving one man. "Henry, why don't you stay here with Mr. Johnson and help Corcoran capture McNabb." Parks gave Washington a big smile, mounted his horse and signaled for the wagon to move off.

"Henry, eh? What's your whole name?"

Marcus Henry, Deputy U.S. Marshal, sir." He flashed Washington a big smile and the huge man liked what he saw. Henry wanted to stay and help in the capture. He was long and thin, wore a heavy Colt in a cross-draw rig and carried a Henry as well.

"I like that. Henry carries a Henry," and Johnson's laugh rumbled across the wide valley. "We'll ride cross-country, Marcus Henry, toward those tunnels." He used his hand to point in the general direction they'd be riding. "In a straight line, probably about five miles or so. It'll be rocky and full of scrub pine, cedar, and sagebrush, so this will be a slow ride."

"These people will be desperate, Mr. Johnson. The ones at the tunnels knowing the wagons didn't make it through, and McNabb, probably knowing that Corcoran is coming up on him."

The riders from the Johnson cabin figured it was just passed the noon hour and at this time of the year they only had about five hours of sunlight at best to make their play. "Once we clear that little ridge out there," Washington said, pointing the way, "we will be able to see where the tunnels are. There'll be a lot of dips and ditches between here and there, though. When we come out from a dip or a ditch, try to come up behind a tree or bush. Maybe we'll be able to get close without being seen."

CHAPTER 17

"HE CAN'T BE BUT HALF A MILE IN FRONT OF US, Terrence. That horse is worthless for a fast ride but he will make it to the tunnels. You have any idea how many men might really be there? Washington said he thought he saw four. We're gonna need back up." Skipper Johnson was as good a tracker as Corcoran and they picked up McNabb's trail as soon as they hit the springs.

"I'm sure there'd be three or four and maybe more. We don't know everyone who was part of the gang in Virginia City and Simpson couldn't tell us since he didn't know any of Jaeckes' gang. It would be best if we can catch McNabb before he reaches the tunnels." Corcoran laughed a bit and said, "You are my back up." Corcoran and Johnson put their horses in a gentle trot eating up the landscape.

McNabb could tell that he wasn't going to make it, Corcoran and whoever was riding with him would soon run him down, probably a mile from his goal. "I'm a sitting duck riding this nag and with these shoes I would be almost helpless on the ground." He muttered the pros and cons for another couple of minutes, continually looking back over his shoulder.

What went wrong? I was so sure we would pull this off. Less than two hours ago I had thousands of dollars, more than I could ever spend. What went wrong? McNabb was the kind of man who would spend the next few years blaming everyone involved except himself for the failure. That is, he would if he lived through this day.

McNabb would never say he picked the wrong partner, but he would say the partner let him down. He would never say his plan to take wagons full of gold and silver was foolish to start with, but would say the plan failed because those around him didn't do their job. Many would say as the years passed, that McNabb was a loser from the start.

He rode down into a washout and when he came up on the other side, he rode into a boulder field. Huge rocks that had tumbled from a cliff a long time ago were strewn across the landscape, most jagged and broken. This wasn't river rock, this was great stones ripped from the mountain and lay waiting for someone or something to snag, puncture, or rip apart.

He jumped from the draft horse and whipped the horse hard, watching it run away through the rocks and juniper bushes. He ducked into the field of rocks diagonally from his original path, and walked as fast as his sore feet would allow. Putting pressure on the injured foot caused the bleeding to start again. He saw huge black clouds moving quickly on a fast wind and knew he would be fighting a blizzard before the hour was out.

McNabb was climbing as well as moving forward, trying to get as much distance as he could from wherever the horse might have gone. He used the big rocks and brush to hide his movements and was making fair time. "Another mile, that's all I need, and I'll have guns to protect me."

In his mind, McNabb had already let go of the gold and could only concentrate on making it to the tunnels and then getting out of the area. He could almost visualize rushing into the general area of the tunnels and being welcomed by armed men, sworn to protect him. He didn't include in his vision the fact that they were promised bags full of gold for that protection.

McNabb's life was spent in an office or at a dining table and this exertion was taking its toll. He was worn down to barely making forward progress and the climbing had ended several minutes ago. Breathing at this altitude was difficult for someone out of condition and McNabb needed to find someplace to make a stand.

Skipper Johnson and Terrence Corcoran climbed out of the deep dry wash into the boulder field and picked up the trail right away. It was after about five minutes that Corcoran held them up. "We gotta go back some, Skipper. He bailed off. We're following an empty saddle."

The tracks they were following wandered about, didn't follow a line. The horse would stop and nibble at some grass, and Corcoran saw it before they had followed too long a time.

They turned back about fifty yards and saw where McNabb had stepped off the horse and picked up the new trail right away. "Shifty little bastard," Skipper chuckled. "He's bleeding, Terrence. Look here," and he pointed at a set of footprints. The footprints showed plainly that the man was limping. The horses moved a lot faster and easier through the rocks than McNabb could, and it was Corcoran who spotted McNabb after about fifteen minutes.

"Just to your left, Skipper," he said, pointing. "There, see him?"

"No rifle, just a sidearm. Want me to pop him?" Johnson said, bringing his Henry up to his shoulder.

"No, I want that fool very much alive. Let's ride him down and shoot him only if it's necessary." Corcoran drew his revolver and nudged old Rube into a gentle trot, closing quickly on the wounded outlaw. *I want to see the look of terror in your eyes, Mr. McNabb, former district attorney. I want you to know that one mistake and I put a bullet between those eyes. But first I'm going to let you tell me about Emilio Locatelli.*

"I ONLY SEE two men out there, Mr. Johnson."

"Might be more in the tunnels, Henry. Let's tie the horses off and go in on foot, slow and quiet like."

Marcus Henry and Washington Johnson were about two hundred yards from the area of the tunnels and used scrub brush and rocks to cover their movement as they slowly worked their way close. Two men were sitting on empty crates near a good fire, shielded from the wind, drinking coffee as the men approached. Deputy U.S. Marshals generally aren't in the habit of simply giving up the command in a situation, but in Deputy Marshal Henry's mind, Washington Johnson, twice Henry's size, was in command.

"I've been in fire fights in Wyoming, Nevada, even

New Mexico," he murmured, following the black giant through the brush. "Damn me, I've never even seen someone as big as Washington Johnson. What would it take to whup a man that size?" He was almost laughing at the thought when he noticed Washington giving him a hard look. He quieted down immediately.

Washington crawled on his belly the last ten yards with Henry following right behind, and nestled under a large sagebrush. They were close enough to hear the men talking.

"IF AIN'T nobody shows up in the next half hour, I'm out of here," one of the two men at the tunnel site said. "Old Jaeckes is crazy as a loon and I don't trust none of them others. Betcha they got their knickers ripped good when they tried to rob that shipment.

"Course that means we ain't gonna get paid, either. We got horses, we ain't committed no kind of crime, let's just high tail it. We don't owe them nothin', Sonny, it's them what owes us." The man was called Wesley Sampson and he stood up, swished his coffee cup clean and headed toward one of the tunnels. The man called Sonny got up to follow.

"Think they'll just ride off?" Washington was almost chuckling watching the two enter a tunnel.

"They could," Henry said. "That one feller was right, they haven't committed a crime that I know of. Sitting on empty crates drinking coffee ain't a crime. Of course, why they were there, that's a different story, but until something happens, it ain't a crime." He settled down into the dirt, a crooked smile on his face. "Let's just sit and watch for a spell.

"Didn't you say you saw four men?"

"Yup, I'm sure there were four. We'd best plan on four guns looking our way when we make our move," Johnson said.

"YOU SWING AROUND to the left, Skipper, and I'll use those rocks there to get up close to him. If you have to shoot him, try not to kill him." He watched Johnson move around some big boulders and crouch down behind a sagebrush. *A big man like that doesn't do a very good job of crouching,* he chuckled.

McNabb was sitting on a rock nursing one of his feet. "Got this far," he muttered. "Just make it around that little cliff there and I should be able to see the tunnels. Sonny and Sampson have horses, food and water. Shoot those dumb bastards and get going fast." He stopped talking and put his ripped-up shoe back on.

"Better not shoot those boys. I'll use my knife, nice and quiet." In his mind, Corcoran and Johnson were off trailing that worn out horse and he was more than startled when Corcoran spoke to him from behind a rock that was less than ten yards away.

"Stand up nice and slow, Mr. District Attorney, and pull that hog-leg just as slow as you can. Let it fall to the ground and you might live to see the inside of the Carson City Prison. Come on now, nice and slow."

McNabb whirled on that rock drawing his revolver but not finding a target. He waved the pistol, looking around in every direction, wanting to shoot something.

A bullet bounced off the rock he was sitting on, splashing gravel into his leg. "Next one goes through your heart, fool," Johnson bawled.

McNabb whirled on the voice but saw nothing to shoot at. What he felt, though, was the butt end of Corcoran's heavy Colt. Lightning flashed through his eyes, his knees buckled, and a big hand ripped the gun out of his hand as he fell face first into the broken rocks around him.

"Nice shooting, Mr. Johnson."

"Thank you, Terrence," Skipper said, walking up to the unconscious McNabb. "He isn't going to enjoy the walk back to my brother's cabin."

"WHAT THE HELL WAS THAT?" Sonny said, spinning at the sound of a rifle shot off in the distance. "Somebody shooting at us?" He pulled his sidearm and walked to the tunnel entrance. There were no other shots, just the one, and the two men stood, guns drawn looking out across the desert.

"Let's get the horses saddled," Sonny said. "I don't like just sittin' around waitin'. I'm all for making it out of here."

"Yeah," is all Wes Sampson said. "Grab out gear, some food, and let's head for Idaho or somewhere."

Henry and Johnson were close enough to hear the conversation and moved up even closer when the two men slipped back in the tunnel to fetch their horse. Washington stood on one side of the portal and Henry on the other and when the two men walked their horses out, called them to a halt.

"Don't either of you make a stupid move and you'll live," Henry said. "I'm Deputy U.S. Marshal Henry. Don't move." Both men froze, holding a lead rope in one hand, and not willing to pull a gun on a marshal. "Good boys," Henry said. Washington slipped the revolver from Sampson's holster and then Sonny's, and told the men to tie their horses off at a hitching rack.

"I'm hoping that shot came from Corcoran," Johnson said. "I'm gonna ride out that way and make sure. You okay holding these two?"

"We'll be fine," Henry smiled. "You two, sit back down on those crates, keep your mouths shut, and everyone will live through all this nonsense." Henry walked over to the little fire the men had and poured himself a cup of coffee, found a crate of his own, and settled down to wait for Johnson to bring back whoever had done the shooting.

"Where are your companions?" Henry asked as he watched Johnson ride off. "Did they bug out on you?"

"Left a couple of hours ago. We should have, too," Sonny said. "We ain't done nothin' wrong, marshal. Why you pointing that gun at us?"

"Maybe you have, maybe you haven't," Henry chuckled. "We'll just have to wait and see."

"SHAME YOU CHASED off that horse you almost killed," Corcoran said. He prodded McNabb to his feet, motioned for Skipper Johnson to mount up, did the same, and used his foot to nudge the handcuffed McNabb into a walk. "You say it's about five miles to your brother's cabin? Just a nice mid-winter stroll, eh Mr. District Attorney?"

Skipper was chuckling taking the lead out of the boulder field toward a little ridge a hundred yards or so in front of them. It was an easy climb out and as they topped the ridge, Skipper gave a wild howl of delight. "Washington Johnson, what are you doing out here in the middle of nowhere?"

"Just came to save your ass, brother," the huge man laughed. "Looks like you and Corcoran have got your man. We've got a couple too. The tunnels are less than a mile back that way. I'll lead," he said and turned his horse to back track. "They even have hot coffee waiting for you."

The ride back was slowed down by McNabb limping bad through the rocks and brush. He whimpered, almost begged, to be given a ride. "My goodness, McNabb, what happened to all that high and mighty arrogance I seem to remember? You better start learning to be tough, cuz the Carson City prison is filled with big bad tough guys just waiting for a little cream puff like you." Corcoran prodded McNabb with his boot at every opportunity.

Marcus Henry stood when the group rode in and took McNabb by the shoulder and shoved him down with Sampson and Sonny. "I assume you all know each other," he said. "Glad it was you doing the shooting," he said to Corcoran. "Think we can make it back to Virginia City before the sun goes down?"

"We'll be running out of daylight but we'll make it. I want a little conversation with McNabb before we leave. Why don't you sit in on it?" They walked over to where the prisoners were seated on crates. "You two, go over and stand with the Johnson brothers, we need to whup on this man you worked for." Sampson and Sonny scuttled over to Skipper and Washington without being told twice.

"Now, Mr. McNabb," Corcoran started, sitting on one of the crates. "Tell me how you, Sheriff Locatelli, and Elon Jaeckes figured you could pull off something as cockeyed as this. This was a failure from the start."

"It was Locatelli's idea. He made me do it, made me bring in Jaeckes."

"I suppose he made you hire Hal Dolan's little gang? Just how stupid do you think I am? I think I know the real story, McNabb, and it would be best if you told it right out."

McNabb wouldn't say anything else. He glared at Corcoran, snuffed at Henry, and lowered his head to look at the ground. "We'll be heading back to town shortly, McNabb," Corcoran said. "Maybe after you've walked a few miles you'll be a little more willing to talk to me."

"I just told you, Corcoran. This is all Locatelli's doing. You talk to your fine sheriff, he'll tell you."

"I'm sure he will," Corcoran chuckled. Corcoran thought he knew what the real story was, but wasn't sure how he would get somebody to actually tell it. There was a lot more to this conspiracy than what he's seen. "A lot of people died today, McNabb, and I'm going to see to it that a judge knows that you are responsible." He stood the man up and shoved him over toward the other prisoners.

"Let's get it moving. McNabb, you cuddle up behind

Sonny there. Skipper, you pony Sampson's horse, and Washington, you pony Sonny's, and Henry, you lead this procession. I'll ride drag." It was a long ride back and very little talk along the way. The icy wind now carried huge snowflakes with it and the sky darkened quickly.

The sun would have been well behind Mt. Davidson, if it could have been seen through the clouds and heavy snow that was falling. The trail in was covered by a couple of inches of fresh snow and got deeper as they went along. The streets of the Comstock were dark, covered in a blanket of icy snow, and the courthouse was lit up like a Roman Candle when they rode in.

"Now that's a welcoming sight," Corcoran said. "Welcome home, McNabb."

CHAPTER 18

"EVENING SHERIFF," CORCORAN SAID. "BROUGHT SOME more guests for your fine little jail. Ah, Marshal McBride, I'm glad you're here, too." He turned to Locatelli and said, "Mr. McNabb seems to think you're behind this effort to steal all that gold and silver. Isn't that right McNabb?"

The sheriff just growled, almost as if he expected to hear what Corcoran said. Terrence walked over to the potbelly stove and poured himself a cup of boiling coffee. During the ride back, Corcoran couldn't make up his mind whether he believed the sheriff was an active participant or was being threatened into taking part in this badly planned robbery attempt. "What do you think, marshal? We know the district attorney is involved up to his neck, so it wouldn't be surprising to find out the sheriff was too?"

"Seems a little out of character on the one hand," McBride said. He slipped up behind Locatelli and quickly lifted the big revolver the sheriff carried. Locatelli tried to spin around to grasp either the weapon or the man. McBride whacked him across the side of the head with the weapon. "But, on the other hand, like you said, Corcoran, the district attorney himself is totally involved."

The subject of a conspiracy led by the district attorney and the sheriff had been discussed while Corcoran was in Carson City, and discussed again in one of the messages sent to the marshal's office. McBride hadn't said anything about the situation until Corcoran brought it up. Corcoran also wondered if the question even had any part to play now that the attempted robbery failed.

Locatelli, blood coursing down his face from the wound blew up, stammering, yelling, stomping his feet, screaming his innocence. "You bastard, McNabb," and he made a lunge at the little man. McBride slammed him on the side of his head, again with his own pistol, sending the heavy Locatelli face first into the floor.

"We'll have none of that," he said. "Corcoran, we need to be alone for a short time and see if we can work this out. I'm sure now there is a conspiracy, but who is conspiring and who isn't, is still up in the air.

"Mr. Parks, Mr. Simpson, and Mr. Henry, will you be kind enough to escort these fine gentleman downstairs? Lock them in separate cells. Keep the sheriff and district attorney as far away from each other as possible." He turned to Corcoran and asked if there was a jailer.

"Old man Conroy usually takes care of our prisoners, Marshal McBride. Isn't he down there?"

"Corcoran, I'm gonna rip you apart," Sheriff Locatelli bawled. "You know I'm not involved in this.

You know it." He was hustled out of the office, and they could hear him cussing Corcoran all the way down to the basement jail. Things quieted down in the office and Parks answered McBride's question.

"Yeah, Conroy's down there," Parks said. "He's been very good getting everyone locked up, getting the doc in to take care of the wounded, and two of the regular daytime deputies are helping him."

"Good," McBride said. "Corcoran, you're now the acting sheriff, I assume. Now is a good time for you and me to go somewhere to have a nice long talk. Parks, you're in charge of the prisoners, and Corcoran just told all the deputies to answer to you until the two of us return." U.S. Marshal McBride knew how to take command and Corcoran had to smile at the way he gave orders. "You okay with that?"

"Yes sir, Marshal McBride, I'm fine with that," he chuckled. His mind was playing with him at this latest turn of events. *First, I shot the sheriff and he fired me and I ran away for a couple of years. Now, I have the sheriff arrested and they make me the acting sheriff. What a strange life I lead. Chasing cows has to make more sense than any of this.*

"I'm very hungry and I know someplace we can talk," Corcoran said. "Has anyone searched Jaeckes' hotel suite? That needs to be done right away. You need to alert your men and my deputies that we don't know if we have captured, wounded, or killed everyone involved in this mess. There may be a couple or more people from the tunnels roaming around, and Jaeckes may have had people on the payroll that I never knew about."

"Have Simpson take care of that," McBride said, and he and Corcoran stepped out into a cold, windy late afternoon. Snow was flying thick and piling up in drifts that would measure in feet before morning. "You think Locatelli had anything to do with this?"

"Not a chance, marshal." Corcoran led them down to C Street and then down the long staircase to the Silver Dollar Hotel Café. "I'm of a different mind on that. McNabb wants us to believe the sheriff is fully involved and has led us down that path for some time, but getting caught in the act, changes the game.

"He will have a difficult time pinning this on Locatelli after being caught with the stolen gold and silver."

They found the restaurant about half filled and Suzanna O'Meara led them to a table apart from the other diners. "I'm glad you weren't involved in all that," she said, waving her arms around some. "All those gunshots. I was afraid for you, Terrence."

"I'm fine, Suzanna," he said. "This is U.S. Marshal McBride and we're both starving to death, dear lady."

She nodded, McBride smiled, and the two men sat down. "Big steaks, lots of potatoes, and hot bread coming up," she said.

Before she could walk away Donald Ferguson walked up to the table and sat down. "And one more," she smiled.

"Looks like all our gold is safe and sound," Ferguson said. "Wells Fargo would like to thank you both for a fine job. I just left the courthouse. You have arrested the sheriff? I'm still not convinced that he was part of the scheme."

"Neither are we," Corcoran said. "There's no paperwork on his arrest, yet, and I'm hoping that we can keep from making it happen. You've been undercover, working daily with McNabb, what do you know that we should know."

"McNabb was a real shyster of an attorney in Chicago and was probably asked to leave town." A definite snicker followed, and Ferguson continued. "He was involved in more than one suspected blackmail situation, and I believe that's what we're looking at here. I think he has something on Locatelli and that's what kept the sheriff from investigating this conspiracy." He sat back and drank from his water glass, nodding slightly before continuing.

"That lack of interest is what you and I have talked about, Terrence." Ferguson took a long drink of coffee and continued. "When you question the sheriff, hammer on that suspicion. When he understands the consequences, he'll be more than happy to tell you all about it."

"If he doesn't shoot me first," Corcoran laughed. "He's really angry right now. First, I shot him, now I've had him arrested. He might not ever want to talk to me again. There's the point though that I've questioned. It's one thing to allow a situation and another to actively participate."

"I think it might be best if the questions come from me," McBride said. "The investigation that you two conducted was impressive, but because of the United States Mint and the Bank of California being involved, this is now a federal criminal investigation. I'm going to ask the federal attorney to have the men removed to the

Carson City Prison for safe keeping and we'll do the interrogations."

"That is probably the best," Donald Ferguson said. "I'm sure Wells Fargo will be pleased with that. The potential loss was huge. I'm sure it will come out eventually, but the dollar amount was in the mid six figures, an amazing potful of money." He was just shaking his head thinking about what the loss might have meant.

"Heard from old man Sharon?" Corcoran was asking about the manager of the Bank of California, William Sharon. Sharon often gave the impression that he believed the bank's money was his money, and was often ruthless in dealing with those not keeping up with loan payments.

"Not a word, neither will you, Mr. Corcoran, and neither will you, Mr. McBride. He's not that kind of feller," and they all snickered over that. "Of course, if they had been even slightly successful, you would still be hearing him from now 'till doomsday."

"I don't want to throw a hammer in the fire, McBride, but how can you move Sheriff Locatelli to the Carson City Prison without him first being charged with a crime? Don't you think we should interrogate him here before any of that takes place?" Corcoran was worried about Locatelli's place in the community. "He's highly respected here, marshal, and this would ruin that if we find out that he's not the least bit involved."

"His not following up on the investigation is a crime, Corcoran. If he was being blackmailed it is not a mitigating circumstance. He's a lawdog, he should have come forward to someone. No, his reputation aside, he committed a crime. By not following the leads that were known, by not investigating this conspiracy to steal from Wells Fargo, people have died. If he wasn't the sheriff, Corcoran, you'd be the first to arrest him."

Corcoran had to chew on that for several minutes and took the opportunity to eat some more, drink some coffee, and look about the restaurant. He smiled at Suzanna, nodded to an acquaintance or two, and finally had to agree with the marshal. "Damn it, I know you're right, I just don't like it. You have to arrest him then, before you can move him to the capital.

"I'd like to have a chance to talk to him, alone, before you have him transferred, if that can be done."

"The transfer can't possibly take place for at least a week, Corcoran, and he is a guest in what is now your jail, so you don't need my permission to question a suspect. All those men are being held on federal charges and will be arraigned in federal court, so none is eligible for bail."

"That will work for me, marshal. I know we did a good job and I'm just uneasy knowing I'm partly responsible for bringing what I consider a good man down. I also know you're right in saying Locatelli, as the sheriff, should have simply arrested McNabb when the blackmail was initiated. He fell for it instead of being an aggressive lawdog."

Supper was concluded with most of an apple pie offered by Suzanna. "I made it fresh this morning, Terrence. I also whipped up some ice cream to go with it." All three men were very quiet for the fifteen minutes it took to eat warm apple pie and the ice cream.

Ferguson and Corcoran walked down C Street toward the Sazerac Saloon and an after-dinner brandy with Michael Donahue. "What a day," is all Corcoran could say when they sat at a table, looking out on a dark main street. He thanked Donahue for the brandy and sipped some, staring out the window.

Snow danced gaily in swirls of the Washoe Zephyr and drifts were forming nicely. By sunrise all traffic in the town would come to a halt except for those with sleighs and sleds. "That little lull between these storms should have given me time to refill the wood box, Terrence," Donahue laughed. "Now, you've put the likes of Tin Cup Duffy or Orin Lathrop out of business, and I'll run out of wood tomorrow."

"I'll see to it you have more than enough wood, my friend." Corcoran said, thinking how different the town would be now that Tin Cup is dead. *He made many people's lives better with his odd jobs, hauling wood, painting porches, shoveling snow. He had a criminal's heart but he did do good work.*

"I'm kind of a devil may care guy, Ferguson. I've got no business being the temporary sheriff and I've got no business questioning Locatelli. I should either be down on D Street partying with the ladies of the night or back at the restaurant flirting with Suzanna. Maybe across the street at the Washoe Club busting up a fight at the faro table."

"Or starting one," Ferguson laughed. Donahue joined in the merriment and Corcoran had to chuckle. "You're one of a kind, Terrence Corcoran," Ferguson said. "You didn't have that badge pinned on for twelve hours before you saw the potential conspiracy, you followed it to a splendid conclusion, saved Wells Fargo tons of money, and got a new job to boot." He sat back, sipped some fine brandy and smiled at the frowning Corcoran.

"Nuts," Corcoran said. He started to say that what he did was what any decent lawman would do and saw the problem "Locatelli simply didn't do his job. I don't know if we'll ever find out what McNabb had on him, but the sheriff was always a strong-willed person so it must be damn serious. Maybe," he said, "we don't want to know."

Deputy Augie Pike walked up to the table, shaking off the cold. "Marshal Parks wants me to take over the night shift, Terrence. He wanted me to tell you that you should get a good night's sleep and be in the office early." Pike eyed the glasses of brandy and Corcoran asked him to sit a spell.

"I won't be sheriff for very long, Augie. I'll have to make a full report of all this to the County Commission and they'll have to call for an election. I won't be running. Spread the word among all the deputies that the job will be open and if they feel they want it, to make themselves known."

"You'd make a fine sheriff, Terrence," Ferguson said. "I'd sure support you."

"I was thinking the same thing about you," Corcoran chuckled. "Virginia City would be hard pressed to find someone more capable."

Augie Pike downed his brandy and stood up. "I'll make my rounds and spread the word. I would be more than willing to support you, Terrence. You'd make a fine sheriff." He looked a bit embarrassed by what he'd said, and hustled out into the cold.

"I'm gonna wander up to the courthouse," Corcoran said. "Maybe have a talk with Parks and Simpson. See you tomorrow, Ferguson."

He made a slight detour into Molinelli's Saloon on his way. "Evening Rathburn. Seems a bit quiet in here tonight."

"You put half my regulars in jail or the hospital, Corcoran," the old barman snarled, but with a wicked little grin on his mug. "Nice work saving that shipment. Guess we know now what all that nonsense was at the brewery, eh?"

"Yup. Old Ike Smithson got tangled up with the wrong people, I'm afraid. Our velvet wearing Hungarian duke turned out to be a Chicago slaughter-house bum, Mr. Rathburn. Just another stupid criminal. I've got a whole jail full of them up there." He had a quick glass of beer and decided it would be better to just go home and get a full night's sleep. *Don't remember when I had a full night's sleep.*

TERRENCE CORCORAN, acting sheriff, sat behind the desk in his office at seven in the morning, coffee boiling away on the potbelly stove, looking over all the reports that had been written following the attempted heist. *Those poor bastards managed to break just about every single law that's ever been written.* He had to chuckle wondering what the young justice of the peace was going to say when he opened court at ten.

Some of the crimes were local jurisdiction crimes,

some were federal crimes, most of those in custody were charged with local and federal. "If the county is smart, they'll let the federal court take first dibs," he said when Deputy U.S. Marshal Enid Parks came in. "It'll save them a bunch of money."

"Even so, they will need to be arraigned. Think we should warn Judge Martin?"

Peter Martin, called One-Eyed Pete by everyone after losing an eye in a mining accident, was just twenty-three years old and had won a special election only three weeks ago following the death of long time JP Louis Spence. "This will be a good wake up call," Corcoran chuckled. "I take it McBride is back in Carson City?"

"Rode back last night along with most of the deputies and Wells Fargo security people. He wants Simpson and me to coordinate most of the activity up here with you. He said this is your jurisdiction and we're here to help."

"Much appreciated, Parks," Corcoran said. "Best bet I guess is to separate the federal and local charges. Almost everyone down in those cells is going to be charged with attempted robbery of a Wells Fargo shipment, attempted murder, and conspiracy to rob a Wells Fargo shipment. Most of those are local. The conspiracy to rob a United States Mint shipment, attempted robbery of a U.S. Mint shipment, and assault and attempted murder of federal officers are of course federal charges.

"I know at least one Wells Fargo officer was wounded. Were any of your people wounded or killed?"

"We had one man take a bullet through his leg and

damn near bled out before they could get to him. He'll survive, but the doc isn't sure he'll have both legs when he leaves the hospital." Both men were shaking their heads thinking about something that horrible. The ravages of leg wounds could be seen every day in veterans from the war between the states. Horribly crippling wounds that seemed to never heal.

"I'll go ahead and write up the local charges," Corcoran said, "and we can take them to One-Eyed Pete this morning. Federal arraignment will have to wait until the suspects are transferred to Carson City, I expect."

"McBride's going to press for a federal judge to come here for the arraignment and order the transfer at the same time," Parks said. "He wants to try to make that happen within the week."

"This place will be a madhouse. We don't even have a district attorney right now. Who will bring these charges? Who will prosecute?"

Corcoran was almost stammering his questions when Sam Owens slipped into the office. "Mornin' Terrence. Here's a wire just came in on our system. It's from Marshal McBride."

"Thanks Sam. Grab some coffee." He read the wire quickly and put it down on the desk. "The assistant prosecutor from Carson City will be arriving on the morning express, Parks, so all my blubbering was wasted." He chuckled, got up, poured more coffee and paced around the office for a minute or so. *I'm not going to let this continue. I'll tell the commissioners they must find someone else and right away. Carrying that piece of tin as a deputy is fine, but I don't ever want to be sheriff. Ever. I'll find me a couple of cows and rope.*

"McBride says his name is Bert Graves. I expect Donald Ferguson will have a bit of explaining to do when Graves arrives, also." Corcoran walked back to the desk and sat down. He opened the drawer on the right and found the sheriff's little flask, still about half full. "Join me, Mr. Parks? Mr. Owens?"

BERT GRAVES WAS in his early fifties, tall and sickly thin, with sallow skin and a balding head. His ears were outsized, his nose was razor sharp, and his eyes watered constantly. He came to Nevada two years ago when his law business in California dried up along with the gold in the near-by creek. The train ride upset his stomach, the high-altitude air on the Comstock made him hard of breath, and he would take these frustrations out on whoever was being charged with whatever crimes he was to prosecute.

Graves had his baggage delivered to the International Hotel and gripping a single satchel hired a buggy for the short but steep ride to the courthouse. His first frustration was finding the district attorney's office locked up, and when he poked his head in the sheriff's office, he found three men drinking whiskey and laughing at something.

"Help you with something, old timer?" Corcoran put his cup down. "Most of the county offices are upstairs."

"I'm Ormsby County Assistant District Attorney Bert Graves, here on temporary assignment. Where would I find a key to the offices across the hall?"

"I'm sure the DA's assistant, Donald Ferguson will be arriving momentarily, Mr. Graves. He usually opens the office around eight thirty. Have a seat. Like some coffee?" Corcoran started to stand up but Parks jumped up and grabbed a cup and the pot. Corcoran said, "The man with the key is behind bars downstairs. Did Marshal McBride give you the background on why you're here?"

"He said if I found Sheriff Corcoran and Deputy U.S. Marshal Parks they would bring me up to date on the problem."

"Well," Corcoran said, "You're lookin' right at 'em. I'm Corcoran, Terrence Corcoran, and this is Deputy Marshal Enid Parks. Like a splash of bourbon in that coffee?"

Bert Graves almost smiled for the first time since his feet hit the cold floor that morning. "I believe that might be in order."

CHAPTER 19

JUSTICE COURT WAS SCHEDULED FOR TEN A.M. AND PETE Martin usually arrived about ten minutes before ten and spent almost three, sometimes four minutes looking at the morning's calendar. "My docket is empty," he would wail when no one was scheduled, and relished the mornings when a drunk or two was to appear before him.

He was astonished to find four men in his office when he arrived. More astonished to learn who the men were. "I've never met a United States Marshal," he said when Enid Parks introduced himself. One-Eyed Pete sat down hard on his swivel chair and stared at the folder full of documents that Bert Graves handed him.

"Attempted murder? Attempted armed robbery? Assault with a deadly weapon? And you're talking about the district attorney and the sheriff?" He was wringing his hands, rocking back and forth in the fragile chair, and looking quickly, that one eye roaming from one to another of the assembled guests.

"You're Mr. Graves?" He said that looking at the

wrong man, and Graves spoke up. One Eye nodded. "You're going to be making these charges then?" He was shaking his head in disbelief. "Will I need to put out a call for a jury?"

"No, judge, this is just the arraignment. This is where you make the decision on whether you have heard enough evidence to hold these men for trial. With the exception of two, all the men will also be facing federal charges. If you decide that the charges should be tried in court, I would suggest that you defer to federal jurisdiction and let the federal court hold their proceedings first." Bert Graves felt better than he had in years, wondering why he hadn't become more serious about being a prosecutor years ago.

I think I could get used to this. I like the idea of a good drink of strong bourbon before court and telling a judge how he should handle the cases before him. Maybe I'll just stick around this rich little town. I'd be hob-nobbing with the nabobs, and he had a hard time holding in the chuckles.

Martin sat back in that old swivel chair, looking about the room as if somebody should speak up and lead him somewhere. "Well, alright then, let's get some little cases out of the way. Sheriff, you'll bring the prisoners in?"

"Yes, they'll be in manacles and surrounded by deputies and federal marshals. I'll have them in your courtroom in fifteen minutes."

One-Eyed Pete slipped into his robes, and with Graves headed for Justice Court while Corcoran and the marshals went down to the jail to gather the prisoners. The prisoners were herded out of their cells, cuffed, and marched upstairs to the courtroom. It was quite a scene when McNabb led the group in.

Martin was still unfamiliar with proper court proceedings and stumbled his way into the arraignment. "Mr. Graves, you will be prosecuting?" Graves nodded and Martin then asked, "Who will be defending these gentlemen?"

McNabb spoke up. "I'm Ezra McNabb, I'll be defending."

"Like hell you will," Locatelli shouted. "I demand my own attorney, and it isn't going to be this bastard."

Before Justice Martin had a chance to quiet things down, three others of the defendants said in loud voices that they too wanted their own attorneys, including Elon Jaeckes. The group was loud and boisterous and Martin had to slam his gavel down several times to get order back.

"Before we can proceed, we will have to sort out who will have representation today. Mr. McNabb, you say you will represent yourself?" McNabb said he would. "And who else will be represented by Mr. McNabb?" Only Ike Smithson said that he would.

"Very well, then," Martin said, sitting a little taller. "Sheriff Corcoran, please escort the prisoners without legal representation back to their cells and we'll proceed with the arraignment of Ezra McNabb and Ike Smithson. In the meantime, we'll take a ten-minute recess."

Martin got up and scurried out of the back of the court and into his chambers. He pulled a bottom drawer open on his old oak desk and lifted a flask of Kentucky's finest. After a solid draught of good bourbon, One-Eye sat down. *What have I got myself into? McNabb used to*

treat me like scum and now, he's on the other side of the room.
What on earth is going on?

Corcoran and his deputies gathered up the rest of the prisoners and got them downstairs. Corcoran was hoping that he would have a chance to talk with Locatelli after he was safely in his cell.

Bert Graves took the extra few minutes to slip into his office and talk to Donald Ferguson. There hadn't been this much activity in the almost new courthouse since it was built, back in '76. "Corcoran tells me that you really aren't McNabb's assistant, that you're a Well Fargo detective?"

"That's right, Mr. Graves. Sent here to investigate rumors or a shipment heist. I won't be able to continue in this office, you understand. I've taken the liberty to put together some names of people in the area that would be able to work as your assistant." He handed Burt Graves a sheet of paper with some names on it.

"Good," Graves said. "Can you at least help me get through this morning?" He was almost begging and Ferguson had the laugh, giving him a nod and a solid whack on the shoulder.

"You bet, boss," he laughed.

"Look, Sheriff, I know you're angry, but we have to talk."

"I'm gonna tear your heart out and blow it up, Corcoran. That's how angry I am. I got nothing to say to you."

"Yes, you have, damn it. What is it that McNabb has on you. What's he holding over your head? What would make a fine lawman like you turn your back on a conspiracy like what was happening? You got a lot to say sheriff and I want to hear it. That U.S. Marshal has you half way to prison, damn it, so talk."

Locatelli stormed around the small cell, just eight feet long and four feet wide, and half of that taken up with a cot bolted to the floor. "I ain't tellin' you Jack. Go to hell, Corcoran." He grabbed the bars and shook them hard enough to rattle cells ten feet away. "McNabb's a filthy sumbitch who should rot in a swamp filled with crocodiles."

The picture brought a chuckle to Corcoran who nodded his full agreement. "Yup, that's not a bad idea." He stood very quietly, looking at Locatelli, begging without saying it, to tell him. He almost whispered, "What's he got on you? What did he find out about you that would make you ignore a crime like this one? Damn it, people died because of all this."

"Bastard knows where my daughter is." Locatelli said it very soft, almost a whisper as well and Corcoran didn't say a word. He wanted to say that he didn't even know that Locatelli had a daughter. Wasn't even aware the man had ever been married. He kept quiet and listened as the sheriff let it all hang out.

"Bertha, my wife, so pretty, so mean and sadistic, left me when little Edith was two and ran off to St. Louis. That was fifteen years ago, Corcoran, and McNabb discovered somehow that Bertha was running a house there. Little Edith was the star attraction.

"He threatened to not just tell the newspaper, he said he has photographs," and Locatelli almost broke down. "Photographs of my little baby ..." and he did break down. He slammed his fist into the steel frame of the bunk, splashing blood over the rough wool blanket. "I'll kill that bastard, Corcoran. I'll kill him."

Corcoran couldn't watch anymore, wasn't going to listen to anymore, and turned to walk out of the cell area. *You might not have to kill McNabb, sheriff. It might just happen one night very soon. I can't keep you out of prison, old friend, because it was your responsibility, but I can help even the score.*

"WELL, Mr. Graves, how was your first day in court?" Corcoran hadn't bothered to go back to the courtroom after his visit with Locatelli. Graves used testimony from the marshals and Ferguson and Corcoran wasn't needed. He spent several hours on the back of Rube, riding up and down the various streets of the town. He spent more than an hour with Skipper Johnson, had lunch with Suzanna O'Meara, even rode down through Slippery Gulch, the nickname for Gold Hill, and finally found himself back at the courthouse.

I'm not capable of doing or even of having done what I believe needs to be done. He had to laugh at what he was trying to get straight in his mind. *McNabb is evil and Locatelli is weak, and it isn't up to me to even the odds or level the table as much as I may want to, which leaves me but one choice.*

"After I put McNabb behind bars for the rest of his life," Graves said, "I'm going to file papers to run for District Attorney right here in Storey County." Graves was pacing around his office and could hear chuckles coming from Corcoran and Ferguson. "Mr. Ferguson has told me about his purpose in being here and will be leaving for other Wells Fargo duties after our trials.

"From what I've seen of his paperwork, he'll be hard to replace. But I guess being a security agent for Wells Fargo is a bit more exciting than being an assistant to the district attorney."

"I'll be moving on, myself," Corcoran said before he ever realized he had already made up his mind. "This old town will never be the same for me after all this. Like you, Ferguson, I'll write a letter to the county commission letting them know I'm resigning my office as soon as these trials are over."

"That's a shame, Terrence," Ferguson said. "You would make a fine sheriff."

"I shot Locatelli once and now I'm sending the man to prison for years. I wouldn't be able to come to work every day in his office, knowing what I know about why he's going to prison." It was that more than anything else that gnawed on Corcoran. McNabb had a picture of Locatelli's daughter working as a whore and was going to offer it to the *Territorial Enterprise*. Corcoran never drew on a man that hadn't drawn first and knew that McNabb would never stand up to him. *Hire the killing? That's what criminals do.*

"McNabb is full of himself," Graves said. "As arrogant a man as I've run into, but not well read on law. Our justice of the peace, old One-Eyed Pete, sat him down several times during the arraignment. He and Ike Smithson were bound over for trial and the federal government immediately put a hold on the two men. The Marshal Service will transport them to the Carson City Prison within the next couple of days." Graves had a satisfied look, finally stopped pacing and sat behind his desk.

"Won't McNabb have to testify at the arraignment of the other defendants?" Corcoran didn't want to lose track of McNabb. Not yet anyway. "I thought McBride was going to get the federal judge up here."

"No, not for arraignment. The federal judge wouldn't agree to coming up here. McNabb would be needed for trial, but the federal trials will go first and the men will have to serve their federal prison terms before any local trial would be held. That may be years and years down the line," Graves said. "Two attorneys from Carson City will be on the morning express, one for Jaeckes and one for the two men at the tunnels that McNabb and Jaeckes hired.

"And Mr. Whiteside, here in town will be representing Locatelli. His hearing will be tomorrow morning." Graves stood up and realized he was not the same man who arrived on the Virginia and Truckee Railroad that morning, and he liked the feeling. "I believe I'll retire to a comfortable position in the friendly confines of a saloon at the hotel. Good evening gentlemen."

"WHERE WILL YOU GO, TERRENCE?" Suzanna was almost in tears when Corcoran told her of his plans to resign as temporary sheriff and leave town.

"I really don't know, dear lady. The only thing I know for certain, I can't stay here. Maybe Austin, maybe Belmont. I know the sheriff in Belmont really well and I'm sure I could hire on there." *Or maybe I'll grab ahol't of you and find a high mountain and just spend my days lovin' on you.*

"You know you're not responsible for putting Mr. Locatelli in prison. He's responsible for that, Terrence. Not you."

"You're right, of course, but I still feel responsible. We fought like hell, called each other bad names, but I had deep feelings for that man. He did wrong, he admitted that to me, but I'm the one sending him to prison. And with his personality, he'll never leave those walls alive.

"There are men in prisons all over the west who are there because of Locatelli. The feds won't protect him, his damn bull-dog personality will prevail at every encounter. I'm going to kill him by sending him to prison." He just stood stock still, shaking his head as if he didn't believe what he was doing, either.

They were slowly walking down B Street after Corcoran helped Suzanna close the café, watching cold winter clouds scud past an almost full moon, sending shadows dancing across the snow and ice sparkling on the streets of the Comstock. "I'm a travelling man, Suzanna, always have been, and I love being a deputy. I would not be a good sheriff."

"You're a good man, Terrence Corcoran, and that's more important than anything. You won't be leaving for at least a week, will you?"

"I'll turn in my resignation tomorrow and leave as soon as the county holds an election to fill the office. Maybe a couple of weeks. We'll always be friends, my lovely." He wanted more than that and so did the lovely Suzanna. He could see tears running down her cheeks and had a hard time holding his own in check. He wanted to spend many years with the lady and knew in his heart he wouldn't.

He couldn't get it out of his head that a settled life was not his. He had never owned property, never even ever lived in a house that he was responsible for, like a rental. How on earth could he ask her to live like that, like a vagabond, not knowing where the next stop would be or what he would be doing when he got there? And he knew he loved the lady.

The walk was quiet for that last half block and neither wanted to say goodnight. Corcoran held her tight, kissed her gently on the forehead, and she slipped into her home.

It was a long and bitter cold walk down Taylor Street to the Sazerac Saloon. The buffalo robe coat was thrown across a chair and Corcoran slumped into an adjoining one. "Just bring the bottle, Michael, and your friendly self." He stretched his long legs out to the side of the table and lit a long thin cigarillo he filched from Locatelli's desk.

"Life is full of shenanigans, eh old friend?" He blew a cloud of blue smoke toward the ceiling, half a smile etched into a craggy face that has aged some in the last few weeks. "I rode up Six Mile Canyon just a few weeks ago, it seems, Brother Donahue, and now I'll be riding back down that long canyon. The world spins on a pointed pyramid of gold and many of those whirling with it have an insatiable greed for that gold."

"It's men like you that keep them from it, Mr. Corcoran, sir. Made any plans?"

"Not a one," he laughed. "I'll draw my wage, pack a

mule, and wander the desert until I find myself. Why did I have to be born with a heart bigger than a brain? That old Marshal McBride, he has a heart made of ice and lead, and will have no lingering thoughts when the iron gates close on Locatelli.

"Those gates haven't creaked an inch and my heart is bleeding like a geyser. What's wrong with me, Michael?"

"You bleed green from the Isles of home, laddy buck, and that will never change. You think like the old troubadour, as a poet would, and carry a gun and an attitude. It's what makes you the man you are, what makes you the friend so many seek. You'll never change and those of us who love you don't want you to." He poured each another full glass of fine Irish whiskey and knew he would have to help Corcoran into the back room in another hour to sleep it off.

Some men are born to wear the badge and shouldn't. He should have been a minstrel, singing his poetry from village to village, dancing with the ladies and breaking hearts at every stop. I'll never have another friend quite like Terrence Corcoran. I always wanted a son, and what wonders if he could be like Terrence Corcoran.

CHAPTER 20

AUGIE PIKE HAD THE POTBELLY STOVE RED HOT WHEN Corcoran arrived at the courthouse. "Anything of serious consequence on the streets of this fine city last night, Augie?" He poured a cup of boiling coffee and settled behind what was now his desk.

"Nice and quiet, Sheriff. The word from the late-night crowd is, they want you to stay. This old town likes a man like you."

Corcoran gave him a gentle smile, sipped some coffee, and ignored the question. "You made up your mind? You'd make a fine sheriff, Mr. Pike. The county clerk will open his office at eight o'clock this morning and I'll hand him my letter of resignation. You might want to hold off going to bed until after I do that, then announce that you will be running for the office."

"It's what I've always wanted, Terrence, but I'd rather you stayed."

"Ain't gonna happen, pard. Putting Locatelli in prison has to happen, Pike. What he did caused several men's lives. It's the why that I couldn't live with. Hope-

229

fully all of that will come out at trial and people will have a better understanding of the man. I'd rather face three men with drawn guns than face what Locatelli did. All because of a mean woman and a back-stabbing bastard of a shyster."

He glanced at the big clock and stood up. "It's time," he muttered, whopped Pike on the shoulder and left for the long climb up the stairs to the county offices. There was a large rotunda at the top of the stairs and when he took the top step he was looking into the district court facilities. The clerk's office was to the left, and he entered at five minutes after eight.

"Fine job you did, Corcoran," County Clerk Virgil Smart said stepping up to the counter. "Did you recover all of the money?"

"Every cent, Virg," he smiled. He slid an envelope onto the counter. "This is my resignation as temporary sheriff. Would you see to it that the commission gets it?"

"You can't resign, Corcoran. We need you."

"The commission will call for an election and you'll have a fine sheriff in that office. And a new district attorney as well," he said. "Let those fine upstanding commissioners know I'll stay until the election, if they'll have me. Don't let them drag their feet, either, Mr. Smart." He left with a slight grin and headed out for another walk around the town.

"ARE YOU SURE OF THAT? I've never even heard the name before." Skipper Johnson was having coffee with his brother, Washington, late in the afternoon. "Penrod. What kind of a name is that?"

"I saw somebody making a cloud of dust at those tunnels and rode over to see what was going on. This one feller called himself Penrod Lathrop and said he was old Orin's brother, come to collect his belongings. He had another man with him, mean looking and wearing a big gun. He never said a word.

"When I asked what they were doing, this Penrod feller told me to mind my own black ass business. I was about to teach him some manners when that second feller's weapon appeared in my face.

"He said if I didn't leave right then, I'd get the same thing that Corcoran was going to get, a bullet in the brain. I left right then thinkin' I'd get that bullet in the back, but all I heard was laughter as I rode off."

"I gotta get the word to Corcoran," Skipper said. "Are those men still out at the tunnels?"

"Far as I know. I ain't been back. Only way I'm going back is with my big old scattergun. If Corcoran wants help, tell him he can count on me," and Washington left the cabin for the long ride back to his cabin in Lousetown.

Skipper Johnson walked up and down D Street and parts of C Street, passing the word that Corcoran needed to talk with him as soon as possible. "Old Lathrop never mentioned anything about a brother. Why would this Penrod be looking to kill Corcoran, it was a U.S. Marshal that blew old Lathrop off that wagon." Skipper was mumbling to himself, walking back to his shack. "Something strange going on."

PENROD LATHROP WAS LIVING in Santa Fe, New Mexico

Territory when he got the letter from his half-brother Orin, telling him about Terrence Corcoran shooting him and the doctor cutting off his right arm. He asked Penrod to come to Virginia City and help him kill the deputy.

Penrod was a known back-shooter in New Mexico and west Texas, and teamed up with another gunman known as Lefty Winston, and rode into Virginia City just two days after the big attempted holdup. Somebody told him the robbers had buried some of the gold at the tunnel site and he and Winston headed out that way.

"Ain't no gold buried out here," Lefty Winston said. "Let's just kill that deputy and get out of town. I don't like this town, I don't like these people, and I'm startin' not to like you." Lefty Winston had no use for another man's life and would take one whether or not he got paid to do it. "I'll kill that fool and you fork over the hundred dollars gold, and I'll be gone."

Penrod Lathrop promised Winston the hundred in gold knowing his brother would be good for it. He wasn't sure how he was going to find one hundred dollars, was pretty sure what Lefty Winston would do if he couldn't come up with the booty.

Lathrop and Winston left the tunnels and rode into Virginia City, planning to make camp somewhere along Seven Mile Canyon, probably near where the two canyons come together. They tied their horses in front of the Washoe Club and walked through the heavy doors, almost bumping into Terrence Corcoran who was about to sit down with Jeb Miner for a cold beer.

"Election's next week, Jim. I'm gonna pack up and light out of here tomorrow morning. Sunrise will see me about half way down Six Mile Canyon, singin' a little ditty my mama taught me."

Miner chuckled knowing that was probably exactly what would be happening. "Wish I could figure out how to go with you, old friend. We do make a pair, you know."

"All you gotta do is make up your mind to do it," Corcoran jibed. "Let Suzanna rent your house, make up a nice pack and tie it onto an angry blue mule, saddle that old nag of yourn, and come with me." He laughed, poked at Miner, and downed his beer. "Gotta go pick up my wages at the courthouse and turn in my badge, Jim. I was laughing, but my offer is real. You'd make a fine saddle partner."

"You hear all that?" Lefty Winston was standing at the bar not five feet from where Corcoran and Miner were sitting. "He just set himself up for us to kill his worthless bones. Let's get down there and make up our camp and set up for to kill him." Lefty Winston lived for opportunities like this; a man simply delivers himself for the slaughter. He could feel his blood boiling, his temples ached with the throb of it, and he had to hold himself in check, to not simply pull that big iron and shoot Corcoran where he sat.

They took down their drinks, bought a bottle and hightailed it out of town and down Six Mile Canyon. Just east of Sugar Loaf Mountain, the canyon splits with the north fork becoming Seven Mile Canyon. There was mining property right at the fork and they camped up the trail from the operation.

"We'll have us a pan full of fried side meat and a glass of whiskey come sunrise, Penrod, and kill us a lawman. You can fork over a hundred in gold, and I hope I never see your sorry face again." He was laughing at his good luck in overhearing what Corcoran said to Jeb Miner.

I gotta get away from this, Lathrop was in a frenzy knowing that he would die right along with Corcoran come the morning. *I'll get him drunk tonight and when he passes out I'll just ride off. What a stupid mess and to think I'm doing it for a half-brother I didn't even like.*

"CORCORAN, wait, hold up, we need to talk." Skipper Johnson was steamrolling down the wooden sidewalk on C Street. "You are hard to find sometimes," he panted.

"Just wanderin' around sayin' my goodbyes, Skipper. Pullin' out in the morning. What's got you in a dither?"

Johnson and Corcoran walked down the street slowly and Skipper told him what Washington had seen and heard at the tunnels. "Did Washington give you any kind of description on this half-brother or his mean looking friend? It would help if I might recognize one of them before they tried to shoot my skinny little butt."

"He said that this Penrod Lathrop didn't look anything like Orin Lathrop, so that isn't a help. He said the mean one was shorter than Lathrop by quite a bit, was very stout, not fat, more like a tree trunk standing there all ugly like. He wasn't wearing a hat and his hair was all curly and hung long onto his shoulders."

"I just saw that man," Corcoran said. "I was talking

with Jeb Miner at the Washoe and those men you just described were standing almost next to me when I told Miner I'd be leaving in the morning. Well, damn me, I bet they'll try an ambush, Mr. Johnson, I bet they will."

"Well, what are you gonna do about it?"

"Probably have to shoot 'em," Corcoran laughed. "I'm getting pretty good at that, you know."

"I'm sick and tired of rancid bacon and wild onions, Lathrop." Lefty Winston stood up near the campfire and threw what was left of his supper into the embers. "Should have bought some good meat while we were in town. And potatoes." He kicked some dirt just because he could and slumped down near his saddle, pulled a bottle of whiskey from the saddlebag and popped the cork.

"We'll kill that deputy in the morning and then I'll resupply for the ride back south," Lathrop said. "You gonna drink that whole bottle? Let me have a taste."

"I bought it, it's mine." He snarled then laughed, and took a long drink from the bottle. "Don't be sniveling. Let me have your cup." Lathrop handed his tin cup over and Winston poured some whiskey in it. "The rest is mine." He laughed long and loud, the effects of the cheap whiskey taking hold.

Lathrop kept the fire going well into the night, watching Winston slowly take the bottle toward the empty mark. Coupled with a hot fire and rotgut whiskey, Lefty Winston was a roaring drunk within half an hour. He sang a bawdy song or two, cussed a five-minute soliloquy at the stars, and rolled into a blanket, dead to the world.

Lathrop gave him five minutes, stoked the fire one last time and slowly rolled up his pack, saddled his horse, mounted, and started to ride out of camp, down toward the junction with Six Mile Canyon.

"Better hold it up right there, Penrod." Winston snarled the name out. "One more step and you're dead." Lathrop heard the hammer click into the cocked position, bent low in the saddle and put the spurs to his horse. Two fast shots rang down the once silent canyon. The drunken Lefty Winston, barely able to stand, his revolver dancing at the end of his arm, sent one bullet plowing into the horse's rear end. He fired again and this one ripped through Lathrop's pack and slammed into his lower back.

The horse collapsed, kicking and squirming, squealing in pain. He kicked up dirt and rocks, his right rear leg not working, doing serious damage to Lathrop's now dead body. Lefty Winston staggered over to the thrashing horse and put two bullets in its head and then one more in Lathrop's head. "Just for good measure," he snickered.

He was in a rage by the time he finished going through Lathrop's meager belongings and not finding a hundred dollars in gold, and after reloading his iron, emptied it into the cold body. "Bastard had no intention of paying me," he screamed, reloading once again. This time he holstered the weapon and rolled his pack. He saddled his horse, took the rifle and scabbard Lathrop had, and rode slowly back toward Virginia City, noticing the sky slowly softening toward sunrise.

"You listen to me, horse," he said. "I'm drunk, cold, and broke, and that means we got to work together," and he giggled a little, hanging on as the horse took a sidestep around a rock in the road. "We gots to kill us somebody that's got some money. People be movin' around soon, so we gots to be quick."

CHAPTER 21

"I'T'S A COLD, COLD MORNING, TERRENCE, BUT YOU WON'T be riding in a storm anyway. Looks to be clear out there." Jeb Miner wanted to ride out with Corcoran but his body told him no in many ways. Those rocks did serious damage and he simply wouldn't be able to ride for days on end.

"Is Skipper Johnson going to ride out of town with you? Two men setting up an ambush, that's about as dangerous as I want to think about."

"He's scoutin' 'em out right now, Jeb." Corcoran had his mule packed well, had some smoked venison meat, coffee, beans, and bacon enough for several days, and was ready to mount up. "I'll come back to town every now and then, just to keep an eye on you, old man," he chuckled. They shook hands and Corcoran stepped into the saddle, nudged old Rube, and rode off.

"Gonna miss that man," Jeb Miner mumbled, walking back into his home and a warm fire. "Wherever he goes things will get exciting."

Corcoran rode down the middle of C Street to Mill

Street and turned east down Six Mile Canyon just as the sun peaked out over the top of Sugar Loaf. As he neared the hospital, Skipper Johnson rode out from behind some cottonwood trees. "You might want to just sit here for a minute, Corcoran," he said. "Your man killed Lathrop and his horse in a drunken rage and should be coming in sight shortly."

He quickly told Corcoran what he'd found at the campsite. "Must have been some party," Corcoran said. "I won't kill him unless I have to, Skipper, and I don't want to have to stick around another day or two. Let's try to take him down and then you ride him up to the courthouse and present him to Mr. Pike. Leave me out of it."

"This is the second time you've ridden off on this old town, Corcoran. I don't much care for it." His thoughts were cut off as they saw Winston slowly riding up out of the canyon, swaying in the saddle and not paying much mind to his surroundings. They let him ride almost abreast of where they were sitting under the cottonwood tree.

"Morning, Mister," Corcoran said, riding quickly out of the shadows. "Keep your hands right where they are and you'll live." Skipper Johnson rode up on Winston's right, but not quickly enough. Winston grabbed for his revolver just as Johnson did.

"Damn fool," Corcoran said. Instead of shooting the burly man, he swung the barrel of his big Colt across the man's head. At the same time, Skipper Johnson knocked Winston's hand away from his revolver, reared back and slammed his huge fist into the man's head as it was knocked toward him.

Between the double blows from Corcoran and Johnson and the lingering effects of bad booze, Lefty Winston toppled head first into the rocks of Mill Street. Johnson was off his horse, lariat in hand and had Winston trussed up in moments.

"Good job, Corcoran. Let's see if we can lift this heavy piece of manure across the saddle." Winston wasn't tall but he was thick, and it took just about everything the two men had to get him across the saddle. Johnson used the ends of the lariat to tie him down. "I'll let Pike worry about getting him off there."

"I'm gonna miss you, Skipper. Give your brother a good knock about and maybe I'll come by this way again, some day." He mounted his horse and watched Skipper Johnson lead Winston's horse back up the steep hill into town. *I don't know yet if I'm gonna miss this town or not.*

He rode out of the canyon and down the Carson River toward Fort Churchill, thinking he would simply follow the old Pony Express trail toward Austin, maybe even further. It was much warmer down in the valley along the river and the ride was a comfortable one. He passed several large ranches but didn't run into any other travelers.

A LOOK AT TERROR ON FLAT TOP RIDGE (TERRENCE CORCORAN BOOK II)

Terrence Corcoran, recovering from injuries he received breaking up a cattle rustling gang, stumbles onto a grisly scene high in the Monitor Range of central Nevada.

That discovery nets him a charming teenage girl from a ranch in the valley, an old army scout who has never lost his abilities, and some wild rides through the Nevada desert in pursuit of Humboldt Charley and a gang of murderers, bank robbers, and kidnappers.

Town marshals protect criminal elements, three county sheriffs become involved, and Corcoran discovers at least one more person from his past is looking to put him six-feet under. It was the robbing of a bank in Belmont that started the problems and the pathetic end to the gang that ended them.

Terror on Flat Top Ridge is a Terrence Corcoran western thriller sure to please.

AVAILABLE NOW

GET YOUR FREE STARTER LIBRARY!

Join the Wolfpack Publishing mailing list for information on new releases, updates, discount offers and your FREE Wolfpack Publishing Starter Library, complete with 5 great western novels:

http://wolfpackpublishing.com/receive-free-wolfpack-publishing-starter-library/

———

Thank you for taking the time to read *Name's Corcoran, Terrence Corcoran*. If you enjoyed it, please consider telling your friends or posting a short review. Word of mouth is an author's best friend and much appreciated.

Thank you.

Johnny Gunn

ABOUT THE AUTHOR

Reno, Nevada novelist, Johnny Gunn, is retired from a long career in journalism. He has worked in print, broadcast, and Internet, including a stint as publisher and editor of the Virginia City Legend. These days, Gunn spends most of his time writing novel length fiction, concentrating on the western genre. Or, you can find him down by the Truckee River with a fly rod in hand.

Gunn and his wife, Patty, live on a small hobby farm about twenty miles north of Reno, sharing space with a couple of horses, some meat rabbits, a flock of chickens, and one crazy goat.